CW00553773

COOK

CONVERSION TABLES

Temperatures

230°C – 450°F – gas mark 8
220°C }
210°C } 425°F – gas mark 7
200°C – 400°F – gas mark 6
190°C – 375°F – gas mark 5
180°C – 350°F – gas mark 4
170°C }
160°C } 325°F – gas mark 3
150°C – 300°F – gas mark 2
140°C – 275°C – gas mark 1
130°C – 250°F – gas mark ½

Weights

30 g – 1 oz
55 g – 2 oz
85 g – 3 oz
110 g – 4 oz
140 g – 5 oz
170 g – 6 oz
200 g – 7 oz
225 g – 8 oz
350 g – 12 oz
450 g – 1 lb
1 kg – 2.25 lb

Liquid Measures

25 ml – 1 fl oz
50 ml – 2 fl oz
75 ml – 3 fl oz
100 ml – 4 fl oz
150 ml – 5 fl oz – ¼ pt
175 ml – 6 fl oz
200 ml – 7 fl oz
225 ml – 8 fl oz
250 ml – 9 fl oz
300 ml – 10 fl oz – ½ pt
600 ml – 20 fl oz – 1 pt
1 litre – 36 fl oz – 1 ¾pts

COOKING FOR BEGINNERS

ELIZA STEPHENS AND ROBERT MUIR

–

WITH AN INTRODUCTION

BY ELEANOR STEPHENS

BLOOMSBURY
in association with
Channel Four Television Corporation

First published in Great Britain 1993
Bloomsbury Publishing Limited,
2 Soho Square, London W1V 5DE

Copyright © 1993 by Eliza Stephens and Robert Muir

The right of Eliza Stephens and Robert Muir to be identified as authors of this work has been asserted in accordance with the Copyright, Designs and Patents Act 1988
Individual writers' contributions including recipes reproduced by permission
Illustrations by Peter Richardson

A CIP catalogue record for this book
is available from the British Library

ISBN 0 7475 1633 2

Based on the television series *Eat Up* produced
for Channel Four Television by Stephens Kerr

Designed by AB3 Design
Typeset by Spectrum City Limited
Printed by Clays Limited, St Ives plc

Contents

Introduction

BY ELEANOR STEPHENS

When I was a child in London in the fifties, my mother, an excellent "plain" cook, made the same meals on every day of the week: Monday was shepherd's pie with left-over meat from Sunday's roast; Tuesday: lamb chops; Wednesday: steak and kidney followed by rice pudding; and so on. Every meal was accompanied by potatoes and vegetables, all cooked for at least half an hour. In later years, she would make spaghetti with grated cheese as an exotic treat, but only when my father and brother weren't around. They wouldn't tolerate that "foreign stuff".

As a teenager, I never saw cooking as anything but a dull chore, a time-consuming activity which kept women chained to the kitchen sink. Along with learning to type, I vowed to avoid it like the plague.

At the age of twenty-two, the year my daughter Eliza was born, I went to study in Boston. I vividly remember the excitement of visiting food markets every Saturday in Boston's Italian quarter and marvelling at the riot of fruit, vegetables, seafood and delicatessen goodies on display.

Fortunately, Eliza's father was a keen cook so we thrived on a tiny budget. She shared his love of cooking and when we moved to Berkeley, California, another region blessed with delicious fresh produce and local wines, it was my daughter and food-loving friends who introduced me to the sensual joys of food. Cooking and eating are pleasures which increase with experience, and the varieties of foods and cuisines to sample seem to multiply each year.

I was, therefore, particularly sad to discover while making our television series *Food File*, that cooking was no longer being taught in most schools. While "Home Economics classes" may conjure up images of children bringing home aptly named "rock cakes", learning to cook is a basic survival skill every young person needs. It is an enjoyable way of learning about scientific principles, history and culture as well as the delights of the senses. I shan't forget the scene we filmed of thirty children at an East London school making all the varieties of bread from their families' country of origin. The boys were particularly proud of their freshly baked nans, pitta and Jewish cholla breads.

Last year the Government announced its commitment to improving the health of the nation. The Department of Health has just given a small sum of money for a project run by the indefatigable Dr Tim Lang to encourage cooking skills in schools. Called Get Cooking, it's a small step in the right direction.

Our recent survey of children's eating habits, commissioned for our Channel 4 children's food series *Eat Up*, makes depressing reading. Many children today live on a diet of sugary, fatty snack foods. Junk food reigns and the two hundred children's food diaries that we analysed revealed that most of the children hardly ever touched any fresh fruit or vegetables at all. It's still chips with everything.

At a time when so many families, particularly single parents, have to survive on such low incomes, it's sad to see that expensive processed foods and snacks take up so much of the weekly shopping basket or pocket money. Cooking your own food can be so much cheaper, better for you and fun – as this book, and the Cook It section in each *Eat Up* programme, demonstrate.

On the brighter side, we know that many young people are increasingly concerned to put right the mess that we've made of looking after the planet and respecting the welfare of our animals and livestock. Research shows that many people would choose organic produce if it were priced more competitively and many, especially younger people, are cutting down their intake of red meat or becoming vegetarian. This book includes a feast of vegetarian dishes as well as plenty for the card-carrying meat-eater.

Eliza and Robert's cookbook takes the reader through a journey of discovery, mastering the essential cooking techniques and skills required to cook delicious, varied meals and maintain a healthy diet. Increasing numbers of young people, especially women, have difficulties with their body image and attitudes to eating. So I'm glad to see that this book resists the current obsession with calorie-counting and slimming diets.

Once you have these Cook It skills at your fingertips, you can choose for yourself whether you want to live on a diet of baked potatoes and pizzas (home-made, we hope) or become the next Claudia Roden. She is one of the ten cookery writers who have donated tips and recipes, specially chosen for their simplicity as well as their deliciousness. We thank them all, and the contributors to our *Eat Up* series who have also given us their recipes.

Eleanor Stephens
Executive Producer *Eat Up*
London 1993

If you wish to support the **Get Cooking** project, you can contact Dr Tim Lang at

THE NATIONAL FOOD ALLIANCE
3rd Floor
5-11 Worship Street
London
EC2A 2BH

1 On the Road to Food Freedom

Learning to cook is like going on a journey. First you have to decide where you want to go and how you want to get there. If you are only interested in catching a jet to a Black Forest Gâteau, this is not the book for you.

This book is a short journey through all the cooking skills and techniques you will need to feed yourself and to make delicious healthy meals for your friends or family. Once you have mastered these basic skills, you will be free to enter the exciting and ever-changing world of food and cooking. You are embarking on a lifelong journey of discovery which will delight and satisfy all your senses.

Almost everyone enjoys eating. We enjoy the tastes, smells, texture and look of food. Sharing a meal together is one of the most satisfying social events in our lives. We all have our individual tastes and our own favourite foods. These are partly dependent on the culture and country we are brought up in. And most people's enjoyment of food expands and develops throughout their lives.

The Chinese say that eating a meal you enjoy actually makes you live longer. When you do something that gives you pleasure, you are happy and relaxed. That's good for your body as well as your mind.
It's lucky that we enjoy eating so much because we have to eat to survive. Our bodies need food to grow strong, to provide energy, to carry out running repairs and to perform all the millions of other activities involved in being alive.

Food is the vital raw material that provides our bodies with the energy and nutrients it needs. Some of these nutrients in food are called **essential nutrients.** They are essential because they must be supplied by food and cannot be made by the body alone. They all have different functions and are found in a wide variety of foods. Some would say that air and water and even love are essential nutrients too!

Variety is the Spice of Life

Although it is important that your body gets all the nutrients it needs, you do not have to worry about this when you are cooking. Just remember this simple slogan: "Variety is the spice of life." In other words, it is important to eat lots of different kinds of food cooked in lots of different ways. For example, tuck in to fried egg and chips one day and your favourite soup with bread the next; a baked potato with tuna salad one day and a Chinese stir-fry with rice the next. It's good to eat some fresh fruit and salad every day.

We have included some tips on diet and health in this book, but as a cook, your most important job is to make your food taste and look as tempting as possible. No matter how nutritious the food you cook, if it tastes bad, it won't get eaten.

You Are What You Eat

Proteins: After water, proteins are the largest group of chemicals in the body. We need protein to grow, to build new cells and to maintain body tissue and muscle. Proteins are made from building blocks, called amino acids, from which these new cells are made. Proteins can also provide energy. The major sources of proteins are meat, fish, dairy products, beans and lentils (called pulses), nuts and seeds. Protein is also found in smaller amounts in bread, pasta, rice and other cereals and grains.

Carbohydrates: Carbohydrates are the body's major source of energy. There are two main kinds: complex carbohydrates and simple sugars. Carbohydrate-rich foods also provide fibre:`

1. Complex carbohydrates are present in starchy foods like potatoes, pasta and bread; they are also found in pulses, vegetables and some fruits like bananas. These types of carbohydrates are slowly broken down and energy is gradually released into the body. These are perfect foods for athletes and for all of us who need a constant source of energy and stamina over a long period of time.

2. Simple sugars appear in several different forms: as sucrose, in refined table sugar, as fructose, in fruit, and as lactose, in milk. Refined sugar is said to contain "empty calories" because it provides energy but no other nutrients. When you eat fruit and milk-sugar, you benefit from the other nutrients found in these foods. Simple sugars are broken down and absorbed very quickly into the body, providing a burst of energy which lasts only for a short time.

3. Fibre: This is the structural material found in plants. Although we can't digest it, it's an important part of the diet. Fibre comes in two forms: the so-called soluble kind, in pulses,

oats and fruits like apples, which seems to slow down our absorption of sugar and cholesterol; and insoluble fibre, in wholegrain cereals and vegetables, which helps to keep the digestive system in good working order.

Fats and oils: Fats can be of animal or vegetable origin and are contained in many foods including meat, dairy products, nuts, seeds and olives. They are concentrated sources of energy and of the fat-soluble vitamins, A, D and E. There are two major groups of fats: saturated and unsaturated. Experts recommend that we reduce the level of saturated fats in our diets because they have been linked to heart disease and high blood pressure. Saturated, hard fats are normally found in animal products like butter, cheese or red meats. Olive oil and some other vegetable oils contain lower levels of saturated fats than animal fats and are better for your health.

Vitamins and Minerals: Vegetables, fruit, nuts, fish, meat, bread, cereals, oils and dairy products all contain different vitamins and minerals. They're everywhere and in small quantities they are essential for good health. Their many different functions include maintaining a healthy nervous system, skin, shiny hair, and an acute sense of taste, smell and sight. Experts now believe that the antioxidant vitamins and minerals like vitamins C and E and beta carotene and the minerals, zinc and selenium, may play an important role in preventing disease. If you eat a varied diet, you don't need to spend money on expensive vitamin pills or food supplements unless advised by your doctor.

2 The Cook It Code

The verb "to cook" means to prepare food ready for eating, especially by the use of heat. Heat causes chemical and physical changes in the structure of the food and can transform a raw food which we wouldn't want to eat into something edible. Animal proteins become harder when heated - see how the slimy, transparent white of an egg changes when it's boiled or fried. Vegetables and grains on the other hand become softer when heated.

So a crucial part of learning to cook is knowing how to control the amount of heat you use. The stove in your kitchen will be either gas or electric. Many people find gas easier to control because you can see the flame: the higher the flame, the greater the heat. With an electric stove you have to rely on the heat indicators on the controls. But you'll soon get used to this with practice and find electric cookers are easier to clean if you spill something!

We have decided not to give instructions for cooking with a microwave oven because we think it's better and more fun to master conventional cooking skills first. And if you are in a hurry to make a meal, you can choose a quick recipe like a stir-fry which can match a microwave for cooking time and tastes much better.

Many people, particularly young people, prefer not to eat meat at all or to eat only chicken and fish. As you will see from the wealth of vegetarian recipes in this book, you don't have to feel deprived if you decide to "go veggie". In fact, a vegetarian diet can open up a whole new world of mouthwatering taste sensations beyond the wildest dreams of meat-eaters. And it certainly isn't bad for you, as Rose Elliot, the vegetarian's guru, explains on page 150.

We have not included many recipes for puddings, cakes and desserts. Most of the dishes we'll be cooking make up satisfying one-course meals which need only some fruit or yoghurt as a second course. If you are a confirmed chocoholic or snack-attacker, we hope we can entice you to try some new mouthwatering flavours that will challenge your taste-buds and inspire you, at least occasionally, to swop the crisps and chocolate bars for a peanut stew or a home-made pizza. So let's Cook It!

Reading the Recipe

1. SERVES FOUR Most recipes are intended for four people or per person.

2. Our recipes indicate three levels of heat when cooking on top of the stove: high, medium and low.

3. All recipes specify oven temperatures in centigrade, fahrenheit and gas mark number, like this :
200°C /400°F/gas mark 6.

4. Weights and measures are given in grammes and ounces, like this:
50 g (2 oz) or 450 g (1 lb).

5. Many recipes specify teaspoon or tablespoon measures. To be really accurate, we suggest you buy a cheap set of plastic measuring spoons.

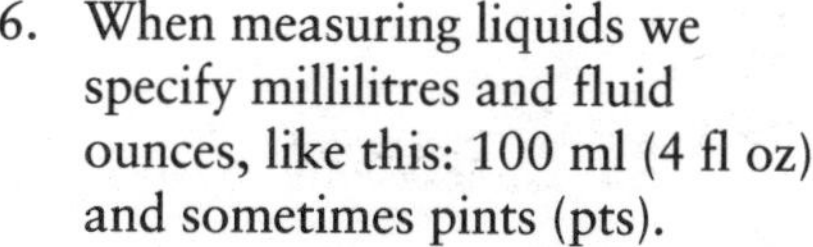

6. When measuring liquids we specify millilitres and fluid ounces, like this: 100 ml (4 fl oz) and sometimes pints (pts).

7. So that you can use other cookbooks, a temperatures, weights and liquids conversion chart is printed on the inside page of the Cook It cover.

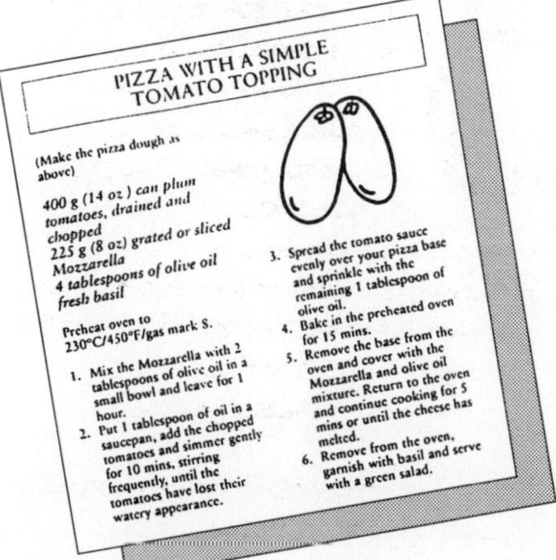

PIZZA WITH A SIMPLE TOMATO TOPPING

(Make the pizza dough as above)

400 g (14 oz) *can plum tomatoes, drained and chopped*
225 g (8 oz) *grated or sliced Mozzarella*
4 *tablespoons of olive oil*
fresh basil

Preheat oven to 230°C/450°F/gas mark 8.

1. Mix the Mozzarella with 2 tablespoons of olive oil in a small bowl and leave for 1 hour.
2. Put 1 tablespoon of oil in a saucepan, add the chopped tomatoes and simmer gently for 10 mins, stirring frequently, until the tomatoes have lost their watery appearance.
3. Spread the tomato sauce evenly over your pizza base and sprinkle with the remaining 1 tablespoon of olive oil.
4. Bake in the preheated oven for 15 mins.
5. Remove the base from the oven and cover with the Mozzarella and olive oil mixture. Return to the oven and continue cooking for 5 mins or until the cheese has melted.
6. Remove from the oven, garnish with basil and serve with a green salad.

All the recipes in *Cook It* are ones that we've tried, tested and enjoyed many times. In Part Two, Global Food, we have included some excellent recipes from various cookery writers we respect. They have kindly let us use some of their simpler recipes which give a flavour of the cooking from their chosen country.

WHY FOLLOW THE RECIPE?

You may hear people boast that they never follow recipes. Our advice is to follow the recipe as closely as possible the first time you make a dish. Otherwise you'll never know how the cookery writer intended it to taste. After that, with experience you can use your own judgement and experiment.

In the end, all recipes are a matter of personal taste and your taste is as valid as the writer's. But when you buy a cookbook, you are buying the cook's years of experience. So why waste it? You wouldn't go to the trouble of buying a map for your journey and then guessing how to get to your destination.

The Cook's Kit

You don't need masses of equipment and gadgets to get cooking. Lots of food can be cooked on an open fire with some silver foil and an old tin can. Most kitchens will have the basic utensils you need: pots and pans, some sharp knives, a chopping board, a cheese grater, a tin opener, wooden spoons, a metal spatula, a sieve and a colander. Many of our recipes use garlic, so you might want to buy a garlic crusher if you don't have one. We've found that "charity" and second-hand shops are excellent sources of cooking equipment.

KNIVES A sharp knife is the single most important part of your cook's kit. There are lots of different knives for different jobs but you can manage with just one or two so long as they are really sharp. Blunt knives are more likely to cause accidents than sharp ones.

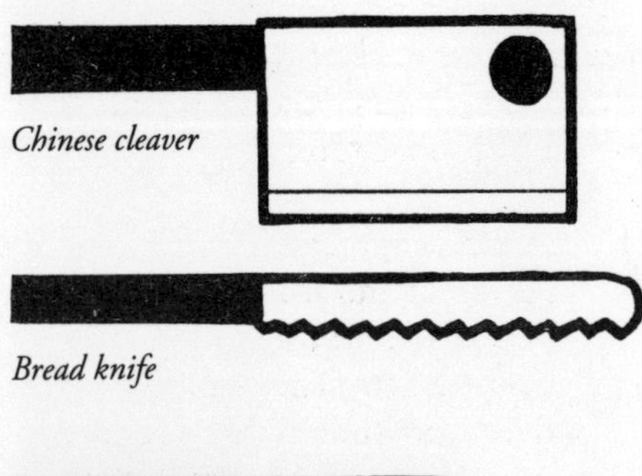

Chinese cleaver

Bread knife

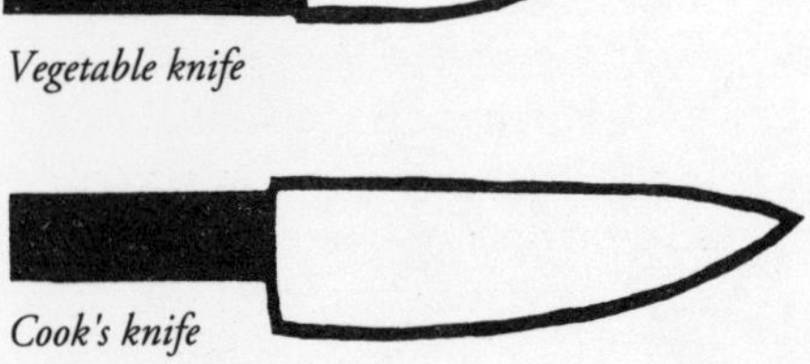

Vegetable knife

Cook's knife

We recommend you buy self-sharpening knives made of stainless steel, such as those in the popular Kitchen Devil range. As you become experienced with handling knives, you might want to buy a Chinese cleaver (illust.) which we find is the most versatile of them all.

Germ Alert

Food hygiene and safety

Good cooks try not to poison their guests or themselves! Germs and bacteria that cause illness can spread very rapidly at room temperature - from just one bacteria to one million in a few hours. Cleanliness and temperature control are the enemies of germs, so try to follow these simple rules:

* Keep yourself and all your cooking utensils and chopping boards as clean as possible. Always wash your hands before you start cooking and after handling raw meat or fish or dirty vegetables.

* Avoid cross contamination by keeping cooked food away from uncooked food, and washing your chopping surface thoroughly after preparing raw meat or fish.

* Don't leave out food that can spoil at room temperature for longer than necessary. Put food in the fridge as soon as it has cooled.

* Always wash vegetables and

fruits in clean water to get rid of dirt, surface chemicals and waxes.

* Take extra care when handling sharp knives, using electrical cooking gadgets (never touch plugs or switches with wet hands), draining hot water, or lifting hot dishes from the stove. Remember that steam can burn skin on contact.

* Hot chilli peppers require special handling. The volatile oils in their flesh and seeds can make your skin tingle and burn your eyes. So avoid touching your face or eyes while using hot chillies and wash your hands with soap and water as soon as you've finished.

* After cooking, always check that you've turned off the stove, oven and other appliances.

* Wash up as you go along. This will make you a popular cook. And remember, the cook never washes up after the meal!

Shop Shop Shop

Shopping is the basis of good cooking. Chefs know that even with years of experience, they can't make a good dish from poor ingredients. So how can you recognise when a fruit is ripe or a fish fresh? We have included basic guidelines for food shopping as we discover different kinds of food.

Most of the ingredients in this book can be found in major supermarkets. But it is worth making friends with your local food traders if you can. And it's good to support them because many, like fishmongers, are dying out, as they become replaced by the big superstores.

1. Your greengrocer. Their vegetables and fruit are often cheaper than those sold in supermarkets. They can also advise you about what's coming into season and what to look forward to.

2. Your butcher. A local family butcher can provide a wealth of information and practical advice. As well as telling you which cuts of meat are best for

which dishes, they will prepare the meat for you, and save you time at home. For example, a butcher can skin and joint a chicken very quickly and will give you the chicken carcass or some cheap bones for your stock-making. They might even have something for the house pet!

3. Your fishmonger. A good fishmonger will sell fresher fish and introduce you to all the ever-increasing varieties of fish.

4. Specialist stores such as Indian, Chinese or Greek-Cypriot shops are invaluable for their spices and other ingredients. For example, fresh bean curd from a Chinese store will taste better and cost less than that sold in supermarket cartons. Because these shops have a faster turnover of spices, their products are usually fresher. And it's good fun to go shopping in a neighbourhood such as Chinatown or in a West Indian market.

5. Healthfood and wholefood shops supply all kinds of pulses, flours, grains and breads as well as fresh herbs and spices. They often have a large range of organic and additive-free foods.

As you become a more experienced and adventurous cook, you will start using less common ingredients, so these last two kinds of stores will become indispensable. Many of their goods are available by mail order catalogue too.

Above all, a shopping expedition can be an adventure. Think of yourself as a detective seeking out the freshest, tastiest, best value (this doesn't mean cheapest) ingredients around. And it's a good form of relaxation too. As the Americans say, "When the going gets tough, the tough go shopping."

The Cook's Cupboard

Some foods are always useful to have around. Here is a list of the foods we like to keep in the cupboard for everyday use:

Vegetable oil and olive oil
Pasta, rice and flour
A selection of dried and canned beans
Tinned tomatoes
Tins of anchovies and tuna fish
Tube or tin of tomato purée
Box of cornflour

Onions and garlic
A bottle of wine vinegar
A pot of Dijon mustard
A bottle of soy sauce
Bay leaves
Dried thyme and dried oregano
Dried red chillies
Black pepper
Sea salt

Planning Your Journey

Before you set out on an expedition, it's wise to sit back and make some plans. Some say this is the best part: While you think about what you want to eat and what you are going to cook, here's a snack to keep you going and to set you off on the Cook It road.

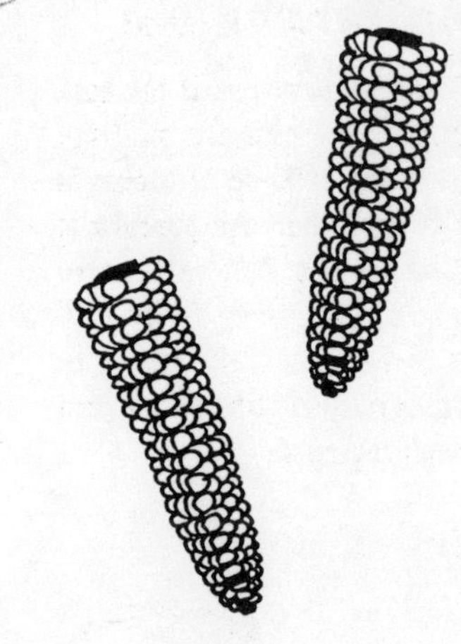

Popcorn

Popcorn is the world's oldest kind of corn. It was a common snack among native American Indians and today is eaten with either salt or sugar by millions of cinema-goers.

POPCORN

1 tablespoon corn oil
popcorn

1. Add the oil to a large saucepan (at least 3-litre volume) with a well-fitting lid.
2. Set over a high heat for 1 min.
3. When the oil is hot, add enough popcorn to cover the bottom of the pan. (The bigger the pan the more popcorn you can use.)
4. Cover the pan and shake continuously until the popping stops (about 5 mins).
5. Transfer your popcorn to a large bowl and prepare the topping.

Who Put the Pop in Popcorn?

The loud pop is the sound of the hard outer shell of the popcorn splitting open due to the build-up of steam in the soft centre when the popcorn is heated. On popping, the soft centre puffs up into a big white fluffy ball. Popcorn increases eight times in volume when popped so be sure to use a big enough saucepan.

POPPING TOPPING

55 g (2 oz) butter
1 tablespoon salt or
2 tablespoons sugar

1. Melt the butter in a small saucepan over a low heat.
2. When melted, add the salt or sugar and mix until dissolved.
3. Pour the butter mixture over the bowl of popcorn and mix thoroughly.

Popcorn is a good alternative to crisps to eat with friends at a party or in front of the telly!

3
Grill It

GRILLING is cooking over or under intense dry heat and is the most ancient of cooking techniques. Barbecuing is a form of grilling, and when people first started cooking they held meat over an open fire. It is one of the quickest and simplest ways of producing a hot meal.

The aim of grilling is to cook the food without losing any of its moisture, and to concentrate the flavours inside the food. This is quite different from making soups or stews when the juices are drawn out to flavour the whole dish.

Many kinds of meat, poultry, fish and vegetables can be grilled. Generally, only good quality meat and fish with a reasonably high fat or oil content can stand straight grilling. Streaky bacon or oily fish like trout are perfect to grill as the fat and oils they contain keep them moist during cooking. Leaner cuts of meat like chicken and most vegetables need to be moistened with oil or butter before grilling.

Another way of preparing meat or fish for grilling or barbecuing is to marinate it first. (Claudia Roden's recipe for Turkish Lamb Kebabs with three different marinades is on page 137).

The grill, with its intense heat source, is perfect for adding finishing touches to cheesy dishes or simply for melting cheese.

CHEESE AND TOMATO ON TOAST

PER PERSON

55 g (2 oz) cheese, grated
1 tomato, sliced
2 slices bread
Freshly ground pepper
Worcestershire sauce

1. Turn on the grill and leave to heat up for a couple of minutes.
2. Place bread under grill and toast on one side. Don't burn it!
3. Remove bread from grill and cover the untoasted side with the slices of tomato and freshly ground pepper.
4. Cover the top with the grated cheese and return to the grill.
5. When cheese has melted, remove from grill. Be careful not to let it burn.

Serve with a few drops of Worcestershire sauce on top.

VARIATIONS

Cheese and pickle on toast: Replace the tomato in the above recipe with sweet pickle.
Cheese and onion on toast: Replace the tomato in the above recipe with thinly sliced onion. (See Chop It on page 34.)

CINNAMON TOAST

A delicious American treat!

1. Make cinnamon sugar by mixing 3 tablespoons of light brown sugar with 1 tablespoon of ground cinnamon.
2. Lightly toast bread on both sides, butter one side and sprinkle with the cinnamon sugar.
3. Toast under grill to melt sugar and eat!

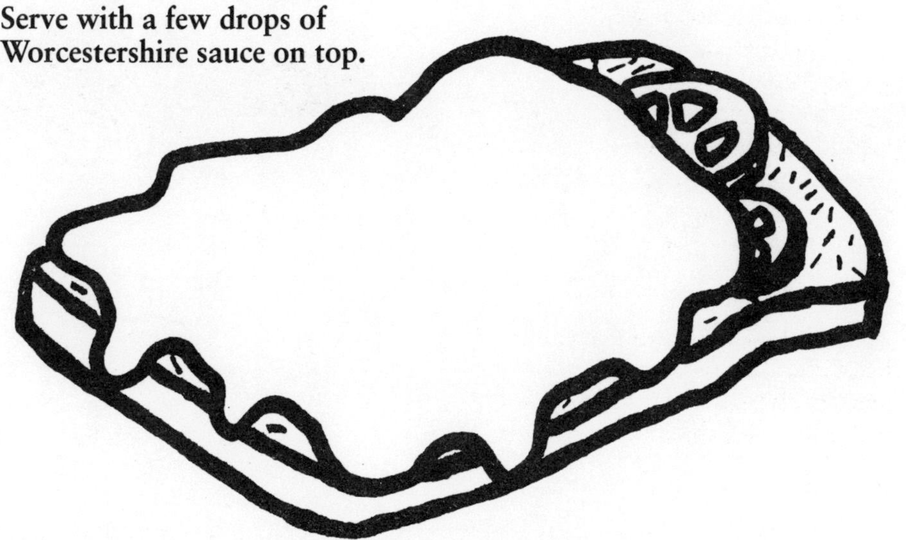

A GRILLED BACON SANDWICH

PER PERSON

2 rashers bacon
2 slices of your favourite bread
butter, margarine or mayonnaise
mustard or ketchup to taste

1. Turn on the grill and leave to heat up for a couple of minutes.
2. Place the bacon rashers on the grill rack and put under the hot grill.
3. Turn the bacon over once during the cooking time. The total cooking time depends on how you like your bacon. The longer you grill it, the crispier it gets. It can burn, so keep an eye on its progress.
4. While the bacon is cooking, spread one side of the bread thinly with butter, margarine or mayonnaise. Add a little mustard or ketchup if you wish.
5. When the bacon is ready, put it between the two slices of bread and enjoy.

VARIATION

Add washed lettuce and some sliced tomato for the classic American "BLT", which stands for Bacon, Lettuce and Tomato.

4
Fry It

FRYING is cooking in hot oil or fat. The oil used in frying can reach very high temperatures and produces food with a good flavour and a crisp, browned surface.

There are two basic methods of frying and these depend on the amount of oil used:

1. The first method uses a frying pan with only enough oil to stop the food from sticking. The French call this “sautéeing” (pronounced “sotaying”). This comes from the word “jump”, because you “jump” or toss the food around in the oil while it’s cooking.
2. The second technique is deep frying which involves completely immersing the food in the hot oil. The oil must be deep enough to allow the food to float. (See Deep Fry It on page 75.)

Frying is quick and simple but requires your care and concentration. The difference between a crispy brown morsel and a burnt offering can be a matter of seconds. So keep an eagle eye on your food when frying. (See the safety rules on page 76.)

Fried Egg on Toast

A famous chef was interviewing new cooks for his kitchen. For their practical test he gave them only one task: to cook a fried egg. Frying an egg is easy to do but it’s worth taking the trouble to do it well.

Fresh eggs are best for frying as fresh egg whites do not spread out like the thin, runny whites of old eggs and the yolk stands high.

FRIED EGG ON TOAST

PER PERSON

1 egg
1 slice of bread, toasted under the grill or in a toaster
2 tablespoons sunflower oil (or of bacon fat)

1. Heat oil in frying pan over a medium heat until hot.
2. Carefully crack the egg against the side of the pan and gently drop the egg into the pan and reduce heat to low. Discard the shell.
3. Cook the egg slowly, occasionally spooning the excess oil over the egg until the white is completely firm.
4. Serve on toast with a little salt and freshly ground black pepper.

VARIATION

Fried eggs are great with grilled tomatoes:
Use 1 tomato per person. Cut it in half and place under a hot grill skin side up. When the skin begins to wrinkle, turn over and cook for another 5 mins. The tomato will take longer to cook than the egg so start it first.

OILS

Edible oils are liquid forms of fat and are considered to be healthier than hard animal fats like lard or butter.

***1. Olive oil:* Superb oil, the colour and taste of Mediterranean sunshine, essential for salad dressings or sprinkled on cooked vegetables. It burns easily so don't use it at very high temperatures. "Extra virgin" comes from the first pressing of the olives. It's the highest quality but more expensive. Buy the best quality olive oil you can afford. Larger bottles are better value.**

***2. Sunflower oil:* All-purpose light oil with very little flavour. Good for cooking or salad dressing.**

***3. Corn oil:* Good for high temperature, deep frying.**

***4. Peanut or ground-nut oil:* Particularly good for Chinese stir-fries. Since it heats to a very high temperature, it can also be used for deep frying.**

5 Boil It

BOILING food in water is another ancient cooking method. Originally water was boiled by dropping stones heated in a fire into a container of water. Later, iron pots were developed which could be heated over the fire, and so cooking with water began.

Several basic cooking methods require water. These include steaming, poaching, making soups, stews and stocks and are all explained in their own sections. The British have a reputation for boiling food to death. Boiled vegetables lose many of their nutrients to the cooking water which is then thrown down the sink. But boiling is vital for cooking rice, pasta and beans.

Pasta

Pasta originally came from Italy but the past few years have seen a pasta revolution in Britain. It's not surprising that it has become so popular. It has a light, chewy texture and can be combined with lots of different sauces. It's quick and easy to cook and supplies the body with lots of long-term energy from starchy carbohydrates.

These days there are lots of varieties of pasta in the shops, both dry and fresh. Fresh pasta is delicious but much more expensive and will keep fresh in the fridge for only a day or two (although it freezes well, too). Dry pasta will keep for months and is an excellent stand-by to keep in your cupboard.

You'll find more pasta recipes, including how to make your own tomato sauces (on page 47) and how to make your own pasta, in Global Food - Italy on page 122.

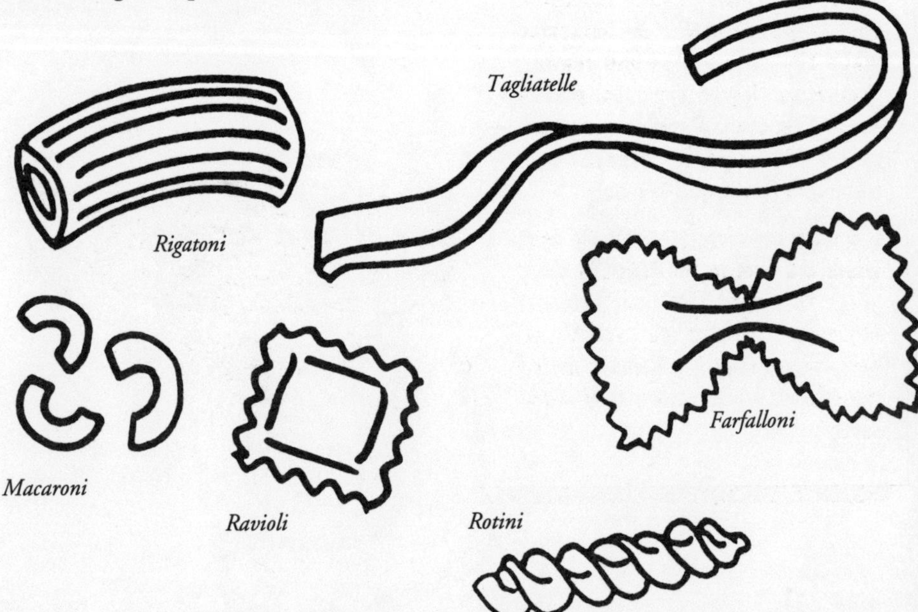

Pasta with Courgettes and Cheese

A very simple, quick meal. The delicate taste of the courgettes really shines through, contrasting with the cheese and black pepper.

To make this recipe, you first need to slice the courgettes into 1 cm (½ in) thick rounds and chop the mozzarella cheese into small cubes. (See Chop It on page 34.)

COURGETTES

Courgettes are members of the marrow family and are native to the Americas. Although they can grow very large, courgettes are harvested when they are young and tender. Courgettes play an important part in the cooking of the Mediterranean, such as in the famous French dish ratatouille (see page 114)

When buying courgettes, choose ones which are firm to the touch, a shiny green colour and without bruises. Although courgettes are available all year round, they are cheaper during the summer months when they are in season.

PASTA WITH COURGETTES AND CHEESE

SERVES FOUR

675 g (1½ lb) courgettes, washed and cut into 1 cm (½ in) round slices
1 packet mozzarella cheese, cut into small cubes
3 tablespoons of olive oil
55 g (2 oz) freshly grated Parmesan cheese
lots of freshly ground black pepper
freshly chopped herbs if you have them

450 g (1 lb) spaghetti or pasta of your choice
1 teaspoon salt (optional)

Cooking the Pasta

1. Bring about 6 pts water to boil in a large saucepan and begin to prepare sauce.
2. As soon as the water is boiling fiercely, add the salt and all the pasta. Feed in the spaghetti slowly so that it bends into the saucepan rather than breaking. Stir once to separate the strands and to stop them sticking together.
3. Bring water quickly back to the boil, and boil briskly in the uncovered pan.
4. Cooking times of pasta vary so follow the timings given on the packet. Check towards the end of the cooking time to make sure it's not overcooked. Your cooked pasta should be firm to the bite not soggy. This texture is known as "al dente". Avoid overcooking!

Note:
If your pasta is too sticky, rinse it under very hot water immediately after cooking.

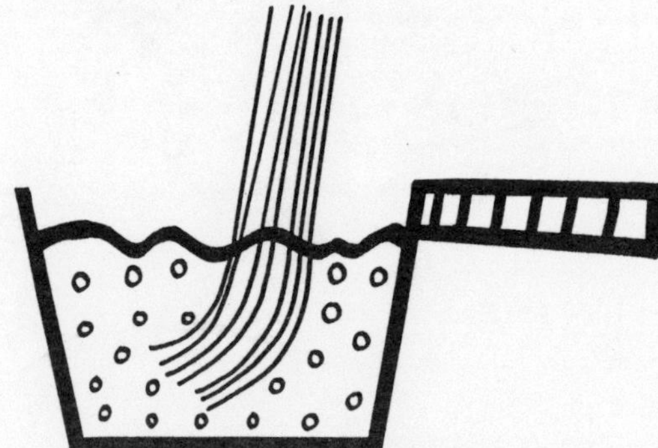

To make the Cheese and Courgette Sauce

1. While the pasta water is coming to the boil, heat the olive oil in a large frying pan over a high heat until the oil is hot.

2. Test that the oil is ready by placing one slice of courgette in the pan. The oil should splutter and bubble at once (but don't let it start to smoke and burn).
3. When the oil is hot, add all the courgettes and, using two large spoons, toss them until they are evenly coated with oil.
4. While the pasta is cooking, toss the courgettes frequently in the frying pan until they are tender and most of them are a light, golden colour. Turn the heat down if the courgettes begin to burn.
5. When the pasta is just cooked *(al dente)* drain it in a colander and return it to the hot pan. Add the diced mozzarella and Parmesan cheese and toss until the mozzarella begins to melt.

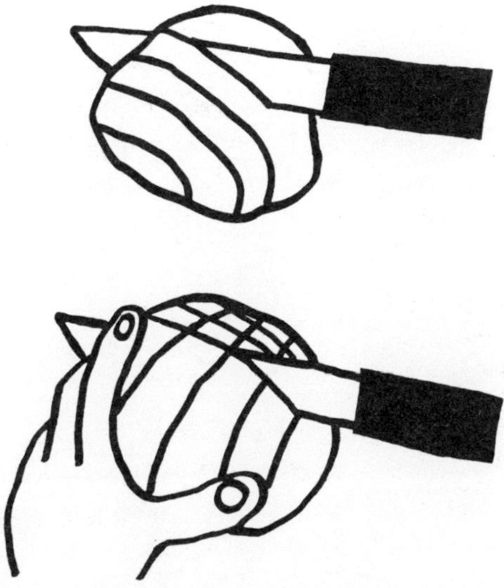

6. Add the courgettes and their cooking oil to the pasta mixture and mix well.
7. Serve straight from the pan or from a preheated serving bowl with lots of freshly ground pepper and some freshly chopped herbs if you have them.

This makes a fine meal served with a green salad and a mustard vinaigrette dressing. (See page 50.)

SALT

We have been using salt since neolithic times. It used to be a very powerful force in the world economy; the word "salary" comes from the ancient Roman word for "salt rations".

Salt is the oldest method of preserving food after freezing and drying, and had the advantage that it could be used to preserve almost anything. Salt was expensive and as a result some foods were thought not to be worth preserving. Hence the phrase still used today: "Not worth their salt".

Salt is necessary for almost every function in our bodies, but only in very small quantities. Many processed foods like crisps are very high in salt. In cooking, salt is used in small quantities to enhance flavour. Be careful not to over-salt the food you cook - a little goes a long way, and too much salt is not good for you. Adding salt or salt and pepper to a dish is known as "seasoning".

6
Chop It

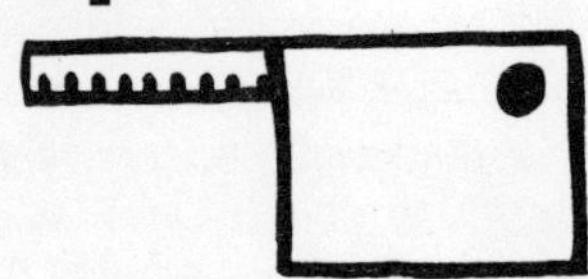

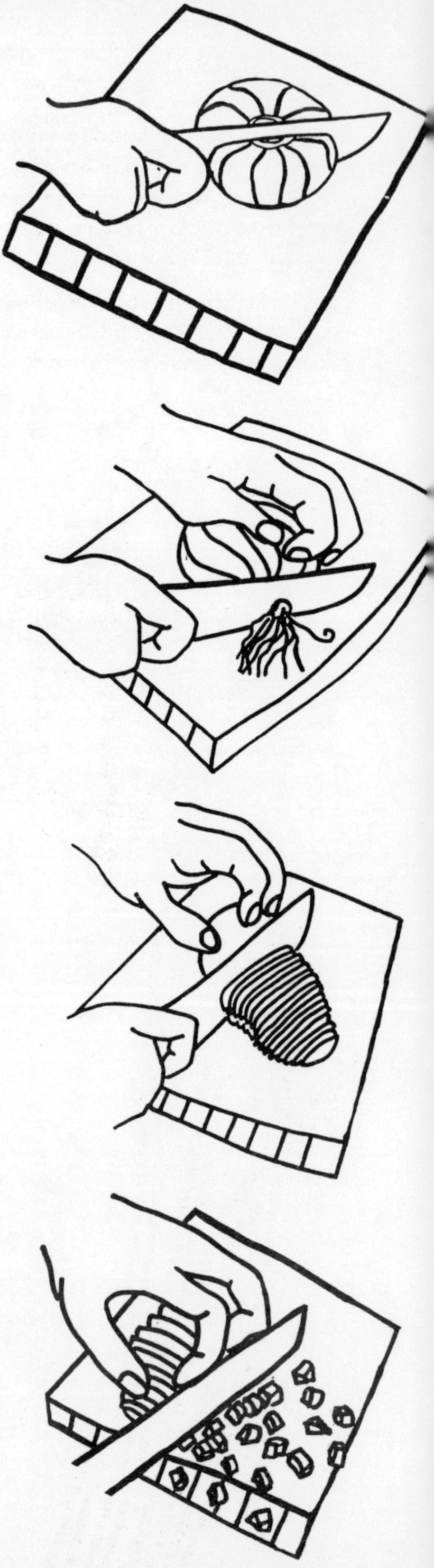

This is where your sharp knife and chopping board come into their own. Food can be chopped into lots of different shapes and sizes for different purposes. Practise your chopping skills on the humble onion, the basis of many of our Cook It recipes.

Chopping an Onion

This can be a boring task but if you follow our quick guide it will only take a minute. Keep the tissues handy!

1. **Top and tail the onion.**
2. **Peel off its outer skin.**
3. **Chop it in half from top to tail.**
4. **Hold the halved onion firmly against the chopping board, cut side down, with your fingertips tucked well away from the knife blade.**
5. **Slice in a straight line from top to bottom as finely as possible. (See diagram.)**
6. **Gather the onion back into one piece, twist it round and chop finely in the other direction. That's it!**

Another excellent recipe to practise your Chop It skills is Gazpacho in Global Food – Spain on page 149.

"Know Your Onions"

The onion has been cultivated for more than five thousand years. There are many different varieties of onion and these can be identified by their colour: yellow, red, white, brown etc. The flavour of onions can vary from strong to sweet. The common yellow onion has a strong flavour which is good for cooking. The red onion has a milder, sweeter flavour and is excellent eaten raw in salads, as are spring onions.

The onion has always been an important source of nutrients and is rich in vitamin C. Onions also contain sulphur which is released during chopping. It is these sulphur vapours that make your eyes water. But it's worth the tears for the flavour.

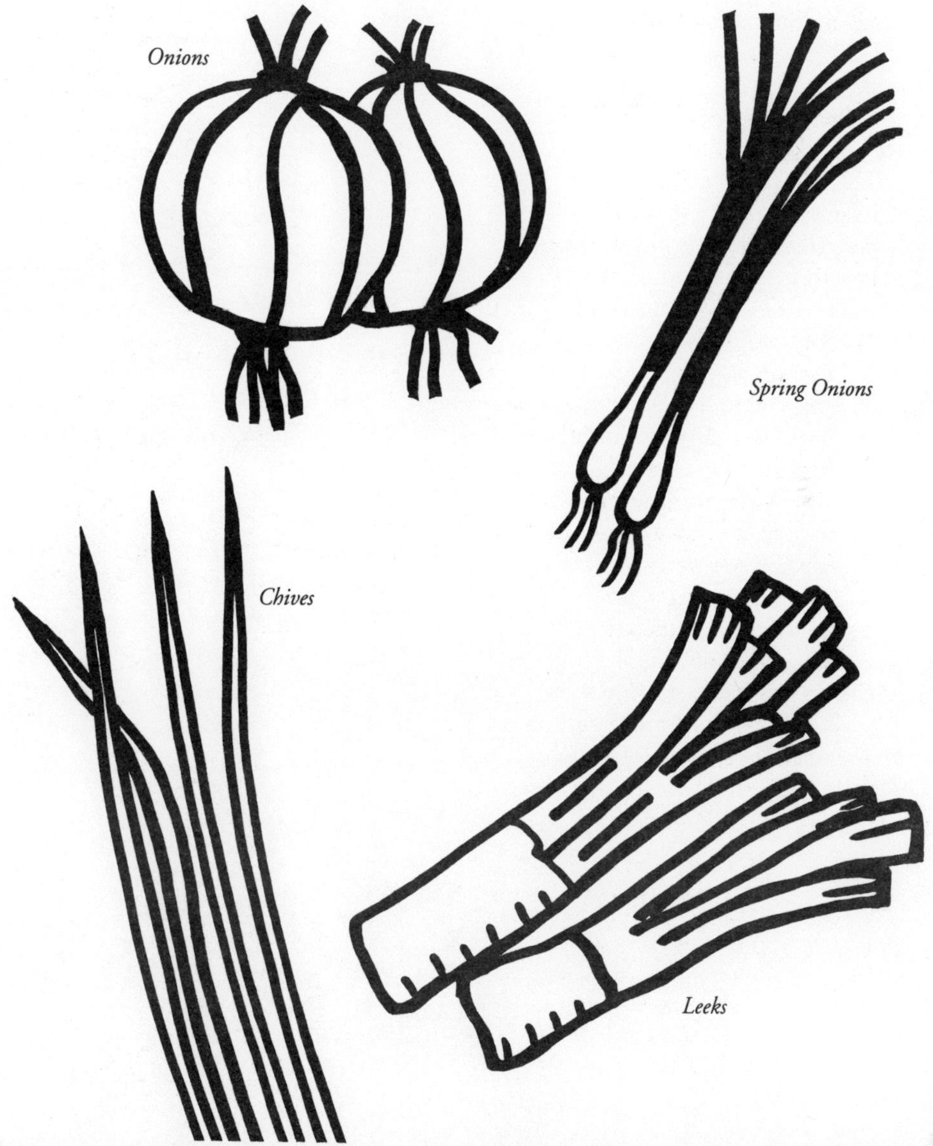

7
Soup It

Making soup is one of life's simple and satisfying pleasures. It provides food for the imagination and fuel for the body. Almost anything can be put into a soup from the simplest vegetables to all kinds of meats and whole fish. Soup can be one of the most economical of all meals and can feed you for several days. It's a particularly good way of using cheaper cuts of meat and left-overs.

Soup-making is excellent for practising your Cook It skills and experimenting with different combinations of textures and flavours.

In soup-making, the cooking water becomes part of the final dish. Less water is used in soup-making than in straight boiling. Some soup recipes suggest using stock instead of water to add extra flavour. (See Take Stock box on page 38.) If you don't have any stock, make up the same quantity of liquid using a good quality stock cube. Choose one which isn't too salty and follow the directions on the packet.

Skill Check for Soup-making

1. SAUTÉEING: frying food rapidly in shallow, hot fat, tossing and turning it until it is evenly browned.
2. SWEATING: cooking gently in oil over a low heat until the food (usually chopped vegetables) is soft and the juices concentrated in the oil.
3. SIMMERING: Cooking in liquid which is heated to just below boiling-point.

COOK IT
ONION SOUP

SOUP

SERVES FOUR

30 g (1 oz) butter
1 tablespoon sunflower oil
450 g (1 lb) onions, thinly sliced
1 tablespoon flour
900 ml ($1\frac{1}{2}$ pts) stock, either meat or vegetable, made from stock cubes (see Take Stock box on page 38)

CROÛTES

6 slices crusty French bread, brown or white, cut about 2.5cm (1in) thick
2 teaspoons olive oil
55 g (2 oz) grated cheese (Cheddar, Gruyère, Parmesan or a mixture)

To make soup

1. Melt the butter and the oil in a large saucepan over a medium heat.
2. Add the onions, stir and cook, uncovered, over a low heat for approx 30 mins, stirring every few minutes, until the onions turn a deep, golden brown and are caramelised. (See box below.)
3. Add the flour and stir constantly for 1 or 2 mins. Remove from heat.
4. Make $1\frac{1}{2}$ pts stock by crumbling the stock cubes into boiling water, following the instructions on the packet.
5. Stir the hot stock into the onions, return the pan to a low heat and simmer, uncovered, for 30 mins.
6. Season with salt and pepper to taste.

To make the Croûtes

1. While the soup simmers, preheat the oven to 170°C/325°F/ gas mark 3.
2. Put the slices of bread on a baking sheet and bake for 15 mins.
3. Remove from the oven and sprinkle both sides of the bread with a little olive oil, turn over and bake again for 15 mins.
4. Pour the soup into a bowl, place a croûte and some grated cheese on top and eat up.

Later, when you have learnt to make your own stock, use this instead and marvel at the difference.

CARAMELISED ONION: When sugar is cooked slowly, it turns a deep, golden brown, the colour of caramel. Surprisingly, some vegetables such as onions contain sugar and when cooked in oil turn a deep, golden brown. They become "caramelised".

Take Stock

Stock is the tasty liquid that remains after other food has been cooked in it. The food (meat, bones, chicken carcasses and vegetables) is gently cooked in water for a couple of hours or more to bring out its flavour and nutrients and to add body and texture. Making stock is a great way of recycling food you might otherwise throw away.

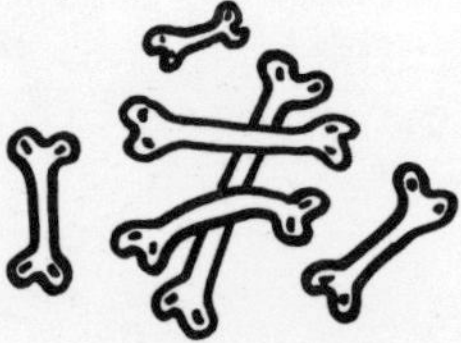

Stocks are used as the basis of many soups and sauces. The flavours of the final dish are built up from the stock's basic flavour. The richest stocks are made from cheap cuts of beef and beef bones. You can also make chicken stocks, fish stocks and vegetable stocks. When a tough cut of meat is used in stock-making, the slow cooking means that the meat becomes tender and can then be used in other dishes. A basic stock recipe is given in Global Food - France.

TONKA LEMON AND LENTIL SOUP

This soup has brought many a young person back to life after a night of wild partying! It's cheap and simple to make, with a delicious lemon tang.

SERVES SIX

1 large onion
1 large carrot
1 potato
3 tablespoons olive oil
2 teaspoons ground coriander
2 cloves garlic, peeled and crushed
225 g (8 oz) brown or green lentils, washed
1.8 litres (3 pts) water
salt and pepper
grated rind (or zest) of a lemon
juice of 1 lemon
1 dried red chilli, broken into pieces
onion, coriander leaves or mint to place on top when serving (garnish)

1. Dice the onion, carrot and potato into small pieces no more than ½in. across. Put in a heavy saucepan with the oil, coriander and garlic.
2. Sweat over a low heat in a covered pan, stirring occasionally, for 15 mins.
3. Add the washed lentils and water, bring to the boil and simmer, uncovered, for an hour.
4. Mash roughly to thicken the soup, add the grated lemon rind and juice and chilli powder, and stir.
5. Serve garnished with thinly sliced onions and chopped coriander or mint.

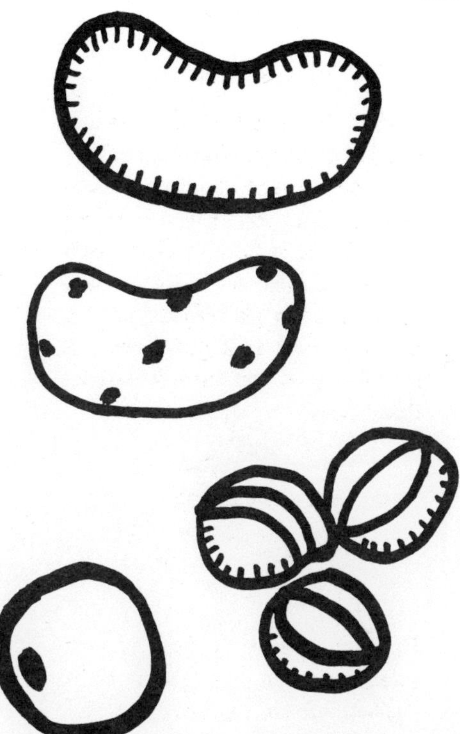

Note:
Measuring of ingredients doesn't have to be spot on for these soups. There is room for improvisation.

Take My Pulse

Pulses are the dried seeds of legumes, like peas, beans and lentils. They are an excellent source of protein and some, like lentils, are high in iron. Pulses have a low water content and when dried can be stored for long periods of time. Beans and pulses require different soaking and cooking times and it's very important to make sure they are thoroughly cooked.

Follow the Flavour Trail

Herbs and spices add flavour, colour and aromas to the food we cook.

HERBS are the leaves of herbaceous plants.

SPICES are the seeds, pods, bark, roots, flowers and fruits of certain plants.

Some plants such as coriander, can be both a herb and a spice. Coriander seeds, as in the recipe above, are a spice and the fresh, tangy coriander leaves are a herb.

Coriander

Spices have been important in shaping world trade and changing world history. Before refrigeration and other modern-day preservation techniques, spices were used to mask the bad flavour of meats that had gone off and to add flavour to over-boiled foods. Spices were also very expensive and their use became a great status symbol. Many wars were fought over the control of spice routes. There are stirring tales of pirates terrorising ships in the Indian Ocean which were laden with spices. At one time, some spices were more expensive than gold.
The supply of spices gradually increased in the fourteenth century when Marco Polo opened new trade routes across Asia. Venice, with its friendly relationship with the Arabs, and their profitable trade in black pepper, soon became the spice centre of Europe. By the beginning of the fifteenth century, Venice had complete control over all spices coming into Europe. The great wealth and status that spices could bring led countries like Spain and Portugal to look for alternative routes. It was on one such voyage that Columbus accidentally discovered the new world of America, together with the tomato, chilli pepper, chocolate and many other foods that were soon to play an important role in the diets of people all over the world.

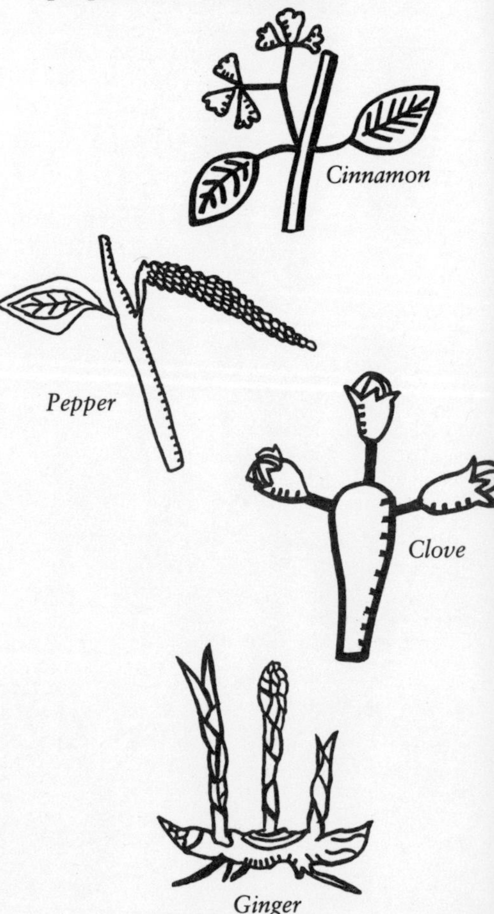

Today refrigeration and modern transport have given us delicately flavoured fresh foods to eat. Herbs and spices are now used to enhance the flavours of foods, not to hide them. Learning to use the different herbs and spices from all over the world is one of the most exciting things a cook can do. Reading cookbooks from different countries and being adventurous in the kitchen is one of the best ways of learning about these magical ingredients.

More information on spices is available in the Global Food - India section.

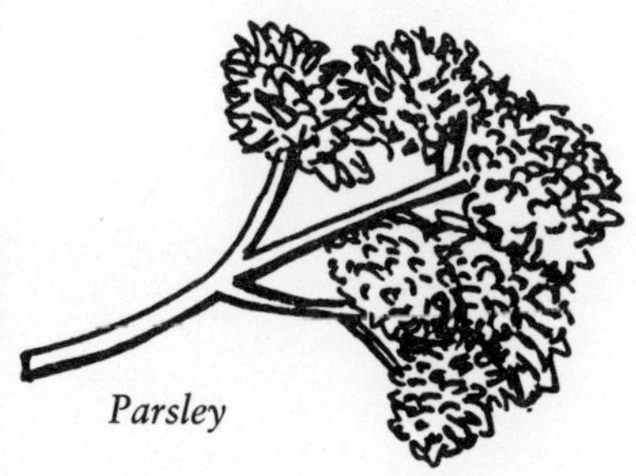

Parsley

Rosemary

Here are some common herbs available in this country. Try growing them from seed in your garden or window-box.

Oregano
- essential in Italian tomato sauce for pizza and also used in other Mediterranean dishes.

Thyme
- used in all Western cuisines and revered in the Caribbean.

Mint
- the English love it with lamb, and in the Middle East it is used in salads and to make mint tea. Also used for flavouring sweets.

Parsley
- the British and North Americans use the curly variety, the Europeans the flat-leaved. Good in sauces, soups or as a garnish. Does not dry well.

Bay leaves
- strongly aromatic - used for flavouring stews, stocks and sauces.

Rosemary
- powerful herb which goes well with roast lamb – just lay a sprig on top while roasting.

Basil
- commonly used in Mediterranean cookery with tomatoes or for pesto sauce. Does not dry well.

Bay leaves

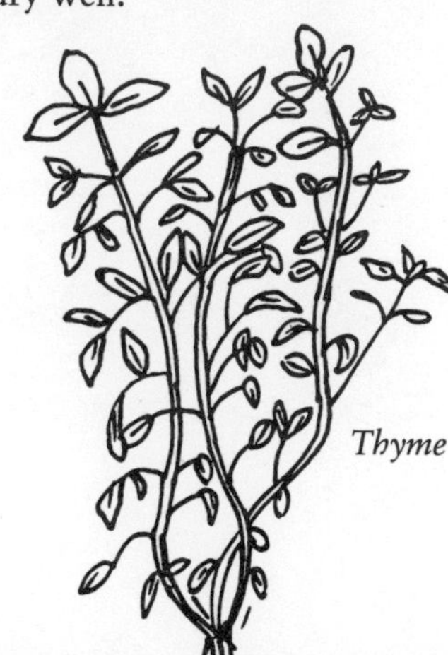

Thyme

8
Poach It

POACHING is the cooking of food in simmering liquid just below boiling point. It's a useful method of cooking delicate foods such as fruits and fish, to prevent them from turning into a mush. When poaching, the liquid should not bubble but shiver gently in one area of the pan. Boiling liquid makes a churning sound, simmering, a peaceful murmur, but poaching should make no noise at all.

Poached Egg on Toast

You can buy egg poachers from kitchen shops but you don't really need one. The technique below works well for a single egg. The whirlpool effect helps to keep the egg white together. If you try poaching an egg exactly the same way but without the whirlpool, you'll see the difference. However, without the whirlpool, more than one egg can be cooked at the same time. Do make sure the egg you use is *very* fresh!

POACHED EGG ON TOAST

1. **Break an egg into a cup.**
2. **Put a litre of water and 1 tablespoon of vinegar into a small saucepan over a high heat.**
3. **When the liquid is barely simmering, turn the heat to low, just to maintain the temperature of the water. Create a whirlpool in the middle of the pan by stirring a spoon quickly around the outer rim of the pan.**
4. **When the whirlpool has formed, drop the egg into the centre.**
5. **Leave the egg to cook (barely simmering) for 2-5 mins depending on whether you wish your yolk to be soft or hard.**
6. **Remove carefully with a slotted spoon, drain off the excess water and serve immediately on toast.**

Poached Fish

Many kinds of fish can be poached successfully in a frying pan or saucepan. You can simmer the fish in various liquids such as water, white wine or milk or make your own fish stock.

SMOKED HADDOCK WITH MUSTARD SAUCE AND MASHED POTATOES

This is a simple way of cooking fish with a tasty sauce. It introduces you to another skill: making a white sauce.

Start by making the mashed potatoes.

Mashed Potatoes

900 g (2 lb) potatoes, scrubbed or peeled and cut into quarters
5 tablespoons milk
15 g (½ oz) butter

1. Add the potatoes to the saucepan of boiling water and cover and cook until very soft. This will take between 15 and 20 mins. While the potatoes are cooking prepare the poached haddock.
2. When very soft, drain the potatoes in a colander and return them to the pan.
3. Add the milk and butter and mash with a potato masher or fork until smooth.

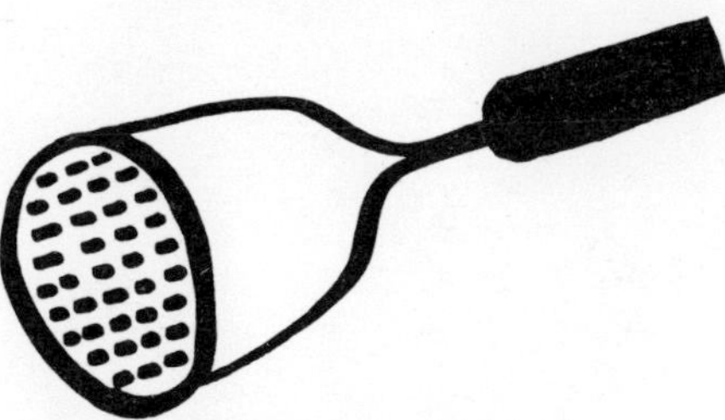

(You would normally add a pinch of salt and pepper but the sauce has a strong flavour from the fish so it's not necessary here.)

Cover pan to keep warm and serve with haddock.

Poaching the Haddock

SERVES FOUR

675 g ($1\frac{1}{2}$ lb) smoked haddock
(6oz per person)
600 ml (1 pt) whole milk
150 ml ($\frac{1}{4}$ pt) water
1 medium onion, roughly sliced
1 bay leaf
30 g (1 oz) butter
1 tablespoon plain flour
1 tablespoon strong mustard, French or English
knob of butter
pepper

1. Put the milk and water into a large frying pan.
2. Add the sliced onion and bay leaf to the milk. Slowly bring this to a gentle boil over a low flame for about 5 mins.
3. Turn down the heat so that the milk is just simmering. Add the haddock pieces, skin side up. Poach for 10 mins on a very low heat until the fish is no longer transparent and is flaky to touch. (Remember to cook very gently. The milk should be barely moving, but not simmering.)
4. When cooked, remove the fish from the milk and place in a covered dish with a few tablespoons of milk. Keep this warm at a very low temperature in the oven. Keep the flavourful poaching milk for making the sauce. The potatoes should now be cooked so mash them ready for serving before making the sauce.

Skill Check

S

Making a Roux
(pronounced "Roo")
A roux is a mixture of butter and flour in equal quantities. It is used to thicken sauces and some soups.

Flour contains a stretchy elastic-like substance called gluten. When you cook flour in hot fat, it glutenises and makes a roux (Flour + Fat = Roux). Adding water, stock or milk to the roux produces a thick sauce. To make a white sauce, the basis of many other sauces, you simply add milk to the roux. (For more sauces, see Global Food - France.)

Mustard Sauce

1. **Using a slotted spoon, remove the onion and bay leaf from the poaching milk and put it into a jug for easy pouring.**
2. **Melt the butter in a saucepan over a low heat, add the flour and stir constantly until the paste turns a light, golden colour. This should take about 1 or 2 mins and is important for cooking the flour and losing its floury taste. This paste is called a roux.**
3. **When the roux is ready, add the poaching milk a little at a time, very slowly, and stir constantly. Follow the pattern of adding a little milk and stirring well until you have a smooth paste and have used all the liquid. This should leave you with a smooth sauce with no lumps.**
4. **When you have added all the milk, add the tablespoon of mustard and bring to a gentle boil for 2-3 mins to thicken the sauce and concentrate the flavour.**

Pour the sauce into a jug and serve with the haddock and mashed potatoes.

VARIATION
Instead of mustard sauce and mashed potatoes, serve the haddock with a poached egg on top and with fresh bread and butter. Some people like to poach the egg in the fish-flavoured milk. Keep the fish warm while the egg poaches.

9
Sauce It

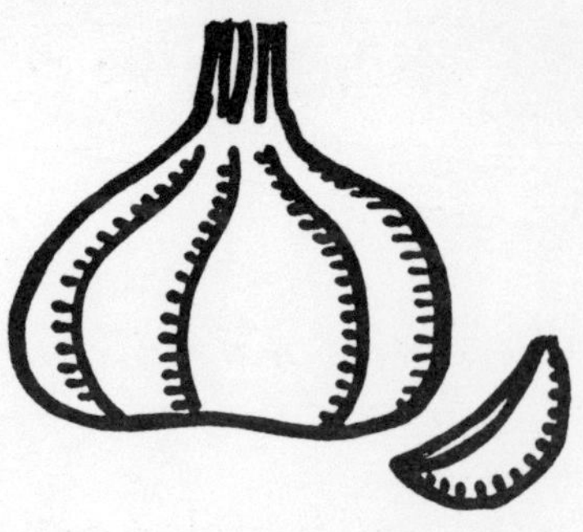

There are thousands of different kinds of sauces. Tomato sauce is probably the most famous and most versatile. Once you can make a good tomato sauce, you have lots of meal choices at your fingertips such as sauces for pasta, as well as toppings for pizzas or for meat or fish dishes. Garlic adds a rich and lively flavour to many sauces.

VAMPIRES BEWARE!

Garlic probably originally came from Asia but the story of garlic began in ancient Egypt, on the mosquito-infested banks of the Nile. Eating garlic stopped the insects from biting and protected against malaria. Workers building the Pyramids were given daily garlic rations. Cutting the workers' garlic allowance led to the first recorded strike in history!

The Romans brought garlic to southern France, which is still the garlic centre of Europe. As well as its magical powers to keep away vampires, its medical powers to help healing are widely accepted. It's even given to the racehorses at Newmarket. It has recently become very popular as a food flavouring and a medicinal cure even in Britain.

BASIC TOMATO AND GARLIC SAUCE

SERVES TWO

2 tablespoons olive oil
1 medium onion, finely chopped
2 cloves garlic, peeled and finely chopped
1 tablespoon tomato purée
400 g (14 oz) can tomatoes
½ teaspoon dried oregano
6 fresh basil leaves, chopped
1 bay leaf
salt and pepper to taste

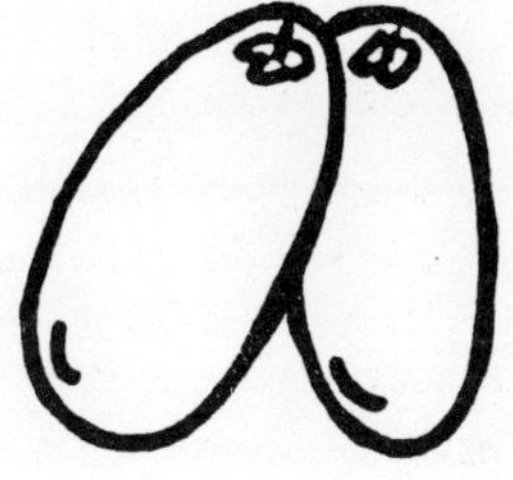

1. Heat the oil in a frying pan over a medium heat for 1 minute.
2. Add the onion and sauté until transparent.
3. Add the garlic and sauté for another minute.
4. Add all the other ingredients, stir, then reduce the heat to low and simmer, uncovered, for 45 mins. Check often. If sauce becomes too dry, add a little water.

VARIATION

Add the contents of a tin of anchovies in olive oil and a washed, diced, red pepper at stage 3 with the garlic. Stir until the anchovies have disappeared - about 2 mins. Continue with stage 4. This doesn't taste fishy but adds an extra richness to the flavour.

BASIC MEAT AND TOMATO SAUCE

SERVES TWO

Follow the recipe for Basic Tomato and Garlic Sauce but add 225 g (½ lb) lean, minced beef just after the onion and garlic are cooked (before step 4). Sauté the meat for about 5 mins until brown, stirring frequently. Then continue as for above recipe.

If you enjoy this dish, go on to make the real thing: a classic Bolognese sauce originally from Bologna in Italy. Any good Italian cookbook will have a recipe for this.

10 Mix It

You'll be popular with everyone if you can make a good salad dressing. And a tasty oil and vinegar dressing doesn't only have to accompany salad vegetables, it's good with pasta and rice too. It's wicked as a sauce for an avocado pear, cut in half with the stone removed, or as a dip for asparagus, artichokes or even hard-boiled eggs. Be a creative salad maker!

The French say that a good salad dressing needs a spendthrift to add the oil, a miser to be stingy with the vinegar and a madman to mix them together.

BASIC VINAIGRETTE DRESSING

2 tablespoons olive oil
1 teaspoon vinegar (white or red wine vinegar)
1/4 teaspoon salt
1/4 teaspoon sugar
1/4 teaspoon pepper, freshly ground if possible

1. **In a dry salad bowl mix together the vinegar, salt, sugar and pepper. Stir well.**
2. **Slowly add the olive oil and mix like mad with a whisk or a fork until the ingredients are well combined.**

This is your basic vinaigrette dressing to which you can add whatever you like. All extra ingredients can be added at stage 1. Our favourite is the mustard vinaigrette described below with the green salad.

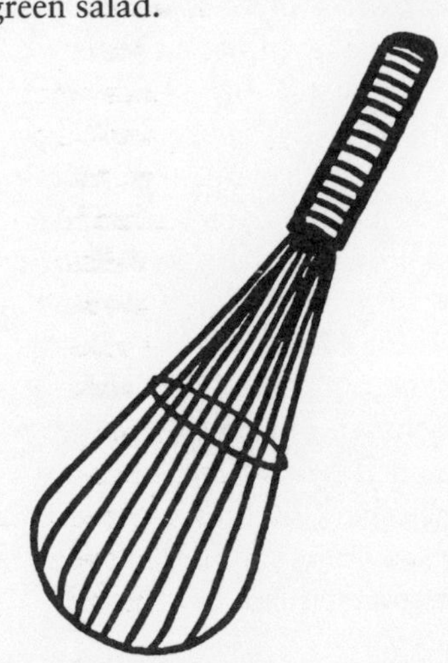

SALAD SECRET

The key to making a good salad is to dry the lettuce after washing. This stops the dressing becoming diluted which can ruin the texture and taste of the salad. There are salad spinners on the market whose only purpose is to dry salad leaves. If you are going to become a frequent salad maker, it's worth investing in one. Otherwise, use a colander. Put the washed salad leaves into the colander. Put a plate that is slightly bigger than the colander over the top like a lid, or cover it tightly with a clean tea towel. Now comes the fun part: go outside and, holding the "lid" firmly, swing the colander up and down until the lettuce is almost dry. Don't soak the neighbours.

Salads

A salad can be a delicious cold meal on its own, with grated or cottage cheese, tuna fish, cold meat etc., or you can eat it as a side dish, making a good meal even better. Until recently, most British salads were extremely dull affairs: a few limp lettuce leaves around large, tasteless chunks of tomato and cucumber, tarted up with a greasy salad cream. It isn't surprising that so many people say they don't like salads. (Our *Eat Up* survey showed that nearly half the young people questioned NEVER ate salads or other veggies.) But now there are so many delicious varieties, it's well worth giving salads another try.

Green Salad

You can use any kind of lettuce or tender, young, green-leafed salad vegetables such as baby spinach or watercress. We love rocket leaves with their nutty, slightly metallic taste. These leaves are ridiculously expensive in shops but are cheap and easy to grow. Some of our favourite lettuces are the round, cos and butterhead varieties. Try them all and experiment with different combinations to see which ones you like best.

THE SALAD BOWL

Any bowl can be used for salads as long as it's big and not made of metal. The acidity of the salad dressing can react with the metal and give it an unpleasant metallic taste.

GREEN SALAD WITH MUSTARD VINAIGRETTE

basic vinaigrette dressing, as above
2 spring onions, thinly sliced
1 clove garlic, peeled and crushed
1 teaspoon Dijon mustard
$^{1}/_{3}$ cucumber, sliced
leaves from 1 lettuce or mixed leaves, washed and dried

1. In a large salad bowl, make the basic vinaigrette following the recipe on page 48. Add the slices of spring onion, crushed garlic and mustard at stage 1. Finish as usual with the olive oil. If you have time, leave the dressing for at least 30 mins to let the flavours mingle.
2. When ready to serve, add the prepared cucumber to the dressing and stir.
3. Add the washed and dried lettuce leaves to the bowl. If the leaves are too big, tear them gently in half with your hands. Don't use a knife as this will bruise the delicate lettuce.
4. JUST before eating, toss the lettuce and dressing together until all the lettuce is evenly covered. This can be done with two large wooden spoons or your clean hands.

VITAMIN C - Why were the Brits called "Limeys"?

British sailors suffered from scurvy, a disease caused by lack of this crucial vitamin in their diet. Limes and lemons are rich in vitamin C, so sailors were made to eat them every day to keep fit during their long months at sea. Hence the nickname!

Vitamin C helps fight infections and keeps the body healthy. It's hard for the body to store it, so you need a daily intake of foods rich in vitamin C such as potatoes, fruit and green vegetables. Alcohol, smoking and stress interfere with your body's ability to absorb vitamin C. So if you have been overdoing it, step up your C intake. Better still, stick to fruit juice and give up the fags!

VITAMIN A - Can you see in the dark?

This vitamin is good for eyesight and all the other senses as well. It keeps skin healthy and can help prevent skin complaints like acne. It also helps protect against polluting chemicals from the atmosphere entering the body. Vitamin A comes from animal products such as liver, and from vegetables such as broccoli and carrots, which are rich in beta carotene.

Darina Allen owns and runs the Ballymaloe Cookery School with her husband Tim in Shanagarry, County Cork, in the Republic of Ireland. Apart from writing may cookbooks and teaching all year round she has also developed extensive herb and fruit gardens around the school. She has given us this salad recipe which uses fruits, herbs and vegetables from her garden.

Darina Allen's Carrot and Apple Salad with Honey and Vinegar Dressing

SERVES SIX as a starter or side salad

This delicious salad can be made in minutes from ingredients you would probably have easily to hand, but it shouldn't be prepared more than half an hour ahead, as the apple will discolour.

DARINA ALLEN'S CARROT AND APPLE SALAD

225 g (8 oz) grated carrot
285 g (10 oz) grated dessert apple, e.g. Cox's Orange Pippin if available

Dressing:
2 good teaspoons Irish honey
1 tablespoon white wine vinegar

Garnish:
a few leaves of lettuce
sprigs of watercress or parsley
chive flowers if you have them

1. Dissolve the honey in the wine vinegar.
2. Mix the coarsely grated carrot and apple together and toss in the sweet and sour dressing.
3. Taste and add a bit more honey or vinegar as required, depending on the sweetness of the apples.

TO SERVE:
Take 6 large side plates – white are best for this. Arrange a few small lettuce leaves on each plate and divide the salad between the plates. Garnish with sprigs of watercress or flat parsley and sprinkle with chive flowers if you have some.

11
Bake It

BAKING is cooking raw food in a heated oven. Making bread is one of the earliest and commonest uses of baking; it converts raw grains into a staple food.

PART ONE
EASY BREAD

WHEAT

This grain is a staple food for 35% of the world's people. Wild wheat is recorded as far back as 8,000 BC in northern Syria. There are now 30,000 varieties of wheat. The three main types are:

HARD - high in protein and used for bread

SOFT - used for cakes and pastry

DURUM - used for pasta, semolina and couscous

Wheat is commonly fed to animals. It takes sixteen pounds of wheat to produce one pound of beef, so meat is a very expensive way to feed people.

EASY BREAD

MAKES TWO LOAVES

1.5 kg (3.3 lb) plain, strong, unbleached flour, brown or white
900 ml (1½pts) lukewarm water
2 tablespoons milk
1 teaspoon sugar
1 level teaspoon salt
1 tablespoon active, dried yeast
2 tablespoons oil

1. In a small bowl put 3 fl oz of the water, add the milk, oil and sugar and stir. Add the yeast and put the mixture in a warm place for 15 mins.
2. In a large bowl, add the flour and salt. Make a well-like hole and to this add a little yeast mixture. Sprinkle the flour over the yeast mixture, cover the bowl and leave for 15 mins.
3. Gradually add the water to the yeast and flour and mix to make a soft, thick mess.
4. Tip the dough on to a floured surface and knead it with the heel of your hands for 10 mins. (See Kneading box on page 54.)
5. Form the dough into a ball, return it to the bowl, cover and leave to rise until it has doubled in size (approximately 1 hr).
6. Tip the dough onto a floured surface and smash the dough with your fist, then divide it into two pieces.
7. Knuckle each piece into a firm, plump cushion.
8. Grease and dust a baking sheet with flour.
9. Turn the round loaves over so that any creases are underneath, place on the baking sheet, cover and leave in a warm place for 20 mins.
10. Preheat oven to 220°C/425°F/gas mark 7.
11. Sprinkle the loaves with flour and bake for 35-40 mins. When cooked, the loaf should be well-risen and crusty and sound hollow when tapped on the bottom.
12. Turn off the oven and dry the loaves upside down in the oven for 5 mins. It's best to let the loaves cool down for an hour before slicing.

Note:
Bread dough can be baked in a loaf tin or moulded into any shape you wish, so use your artistic vision.

WHY DOES BREAD RISE?

Yeast is a tiny organism that can only be seen under a microscope. It feeds on carbohydrates and, given the right environment of warmth, food and moisture, it will produce carbon dioxide. This gas makes the dough puff up or rise - the process is known as "proving".

IF YOU KNEAD IT – PROVE IT

KNEADING strengthens the gluten in the flour and makes your dough smoother and softer or more elastic by incorporating more air into the mixture. Kneading is great fun and very good exercise! Follow these simple steps:

1. Push down on the ball of dough with the heel of one hand and push away from your body.

2. Turn the dough a quarter of a circle.

3. Push down again and repeat stages 1 and 2, turning and pushing down until the dough feels elastic and doesn't stick to the board or to your fingers. This will take about 10 mins - you can knead dough too little but never too much.

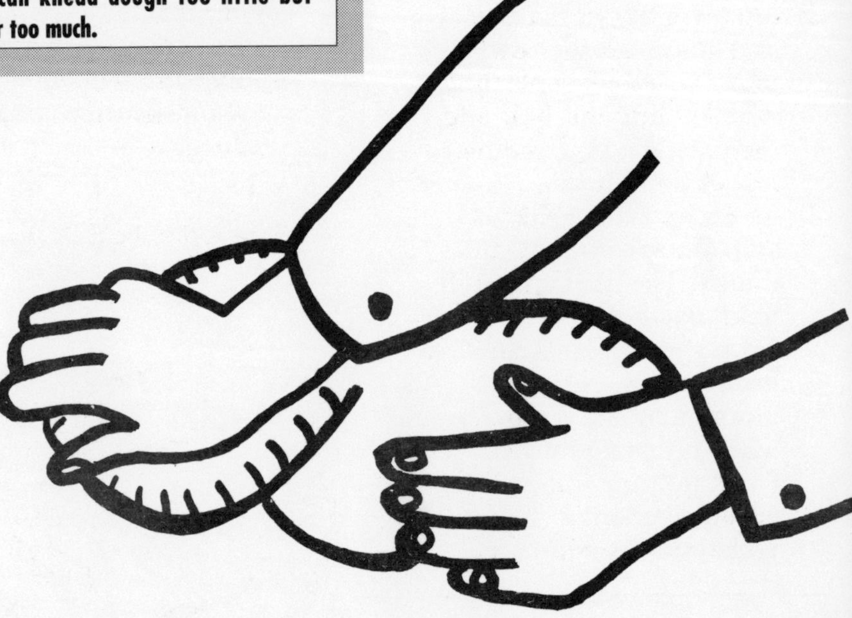

PART TWO PIZZA

PIZZA DOUGH

SERVES FOUR

2 teaspoons active, dried yeast
225 ml (8 fl oz) lukewarm water
450 g (1 lb) unbleached flour
3 tablespoons extra virgin olive oil
1 teaspoon sugar
½ teaspoon salt

1. Put the yeast in a small bowl with 2 fl oz water, 2 tablespoons of oil and 1 teaspoon of sugar. Gently stir and leave to dissolve for 10 mins in a warm place.
2. Meanwhile, put the flour and salt in a large bowl and make a well-like hole in the middle. Into this hole add the yeast mixture and the rest of the water.
3. Mix together to make a soft, flexible but not sticky, dough. The dough should hold together and leave the sides of the bowl clean. If it is too sticky, add a little more flour, if it is too dry, add a little more water. Extra flour or water should be added about 1 tablespoon at a time.
4. Take the dough out of the bowl and slap it down on to a clean, lightly floured work surface several times. Knead it with your fists for about 10 mins (see box) and form into a ball shape.
5. Rub the surface of a clean, dry bowl with 1 teaspoon of oil and place the dough into it. Cover the bowl with a clean tea towel, put it in a dry, warm place, and leave the dough to rise until it has doubled in size, approximately 1 hr.
6. On the lightly floured surface, roll out the dough to the size you want.
7. Transfer it to a greased baking tray.
8. Now add your favourite topping and follow the baking instructions on the next page.

Note:
Never use a glass bottle instead of a rolling pin. It could break, cutting your hands and ruining your dough!

PIZZA WITH A SIMPLE TOMATO TOPPING

(Make the pizza dough as above)

400 g (14 oz) can plum tomatoes, drained and chopped
225 g (8 oz) grated or sliced mozzarella
4 tablespoons olive oil
fresh basil

Preheat oven to 230°C/450°F/gas mark 8.

1. Mix the mozzarella with 2 tablespoons of olive oil in a small bowl and leave for 1 hr.
2. Put 1 tablespoon of oil in a saucepan, add the chopped tomatoes and simmer gently for 10 mins, stirring frequently, until the tomatoes have lost their watery appearance.

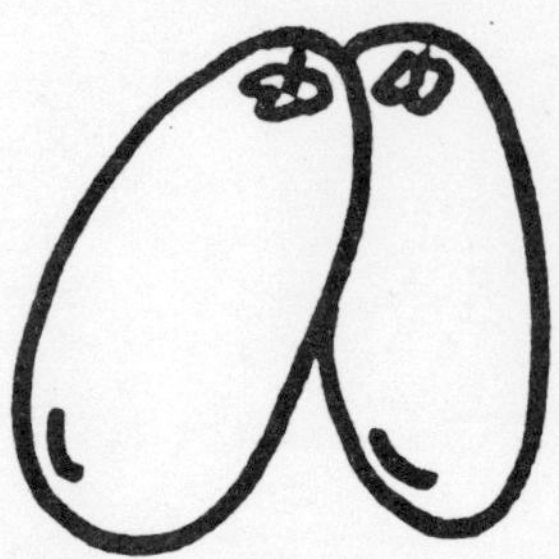

3. Spread the tomato sauce evenly over your pizza base and sprinkle with the remaining tablespoon of olive oil.
4. Bake in the preheated oven for 15 mins.
5. Remove the base from the oven and cover with the mozzarella and olive oil mixture. Return to the oven and continue cooking for 5 mins or until the cheese has melted.
6. Remove from the oven, garnish with basil and serve with a green salad.

PIZZA TOPPINGS

What you put on your pizza is up to you. Feel free to experiment. Most cooks start with a tomato base and put different ingredients on top. If you don't like tomatoes, brush your pizza base with some olive oil and build up from that. But the tomato base provides moisture so choose nice juicy toppings instead.

We have already given two basic tomato sauces for your pizza base.

1. Simple tomato topping in the recipe on page 56. This has a lighter tomato taste and is very quick and easy to make.
2. The basic tomato and garlic sauce on pag 47. This gives your pizza a stronger tomato and herby taste.

Here are some topping suggestions to inspire you. The sky's the limit!

tuna fish, prawns, anchovies or sardines
olives, capers, garlic or onions
fresh chillies for a hot pizza
red and green bell peppers,
artichoke hearts, mushrooms
ham, salami, pepperoni or sausage slices
raisins, pine nuts or pineapple chunks for a sweeter taste
egg - just break a raw egg on to the middle of your pizza and cook
fresh basil, oregano or other herbs and spices

Finish with the usual topping of mozzarella cheese or finely grated Parmesan or both.

PART THREE BAKED POTATOES

Potatoes originally came from Peru and reached Europe in the sixteenth century. They are a staple food and a great source of energy because they are rich in starchy carbohydrates. A baked potato can be eaten as a meal in itself with a sauce or topping or as a side vegetable.

BAKED POTATOES

SERVES ONE

1 large potato
oil

Preheat oven to 230°C/450°F/gas mark 8.

1. **Scrub the potato, prick it with a fork all over and brush with a little oil.**
2. **Place it on a shelf in the middle of the oven and bake for 45 mins or until it is soft (squeeze it a little to check).**
3. **When cooked, slice in half and add a little butter or olive oil.**
4. **You can top it with grated or cottage cheese, tomato and garlic sauce or chilli con carne (see page 86.)**

PART FOUR
FISH

Fish can be divided into three main types: white, oily and shellfish:

White fish includes cod, haddock and plaice.
Oily fish includes mackerel, herring, salmon and trout.
Shellfish includes crabs, mussels, prawns, clams, oysters and lobsters.

All fish are rich in protein and vitamin B, and oily fish also contain large amounts of vitamin D and essential oils. Fresh fish is such a healthy food that it's sometimes called "brain food". So get fishing!

BAKED RAINBOW TROUT

SERVES FOUR
4 rainbow trout (about 225 g or 8 oz each)
2 tablespoons olive oil
salt
pepper
fresh herbs (parsley, chives or fennel)
1 lemon, thinly sliced

Preheat oven to 180°C/350°F/gas mark 4.

1. Wash the trout and wipe dry with kitchen paper.
2. Season the inside with a little salt and pepper and put in the chopped herbs.
3. Cut enough foil to hold the fish plus a bit extra.
4. Brush the foil with oil and place the trout in the middle with 2 thin slices of lemon

Fresh Fish or Foul?

A fresh fish should smell fresh and have glistening skin and firm flesh. Its gills should be bright red and its eyes bright and shiny, not dull or filmy. Fresh fish should always be cooked on the day you buy it. Ask the fishmonger to gut and clean the fish and always wash and dry it before cooking. Bad fish can make you very sick.

on top.

5. Bring the sides of the foil up and scrunch together to seal the package. Leave room for the hot air to circulate in the parcel.
6. Place on a baking sheet and bake for 20-25 mins in the hot oven.
7. Remove from foil on to a warm serving plate when cooked. The flesh should be soft and come easily off the bone. Serve with a garnish of herbs and more lemon, if desired.

Note:
Baked trout served with a baked potato and green salad makes a delicious and nutritious meal.

PART FIVE
EARTHQUAKE CAKE – CHOCOLATE

This cake is divine. It's extremely rich and should serve at least ten people. If you eat too much, it really could be "Death by Chocolate". You have been warned!

EARTHQUAKE CAKE – CHOCOLATE

170 g (6 oz) unsalted butter
110 g (4 oz) plain cooking chocolate
4 eggs
225 g (8 oz) sugar
2 teaspoons natural vanilla essence
140 g (5 oz) plain flour

FROSTING
85 g (3 oz) plain chocolate
1 tablespoon butter
3 tablespoons strong coffee
55 g (2 oz) crushed hazelnuts

Preheat oven to 350°C/180°F/gas mark 4. Butter a 9 x 4in round baking tin.

1. Melt the butter and cooking chocolate in a small saucepan over a low heat. Stir constantly until the mixture is smooth and well

blended. Turn off the heat and leave to cool.

2. Break the eggs into a large mixing bowl and beat with a whisk until light and frothy.
3. Slowly beat in the sugar, a little at a time. The mixture will become pale and thick.
4. Gently and slowly blend the smooth chocolate mixture and vanilla essence into the egg and sugar mixture.
5. Sift the flour through a sieve into the chocolate mix. Gently blend in the flour, mixing as little as possible.
5. Carefully pour the chocolate mixture into the prepared baking tin.
6. Bake the cake for 30-40 mins until the top begins to crack like an earthquake and is firm to the touch. (Be patient.)
7. Remove the cake from the oven and leave it to cool in its tin.
8. Make the frosting by melting the chocolate, coffee and butter in a small saucepan over a low heat. When smooth, turn off the heat.
9. When the cake is cool, run a sharp knife around the edge of the pan and carefully remove the cake. Place it on a serving plate.
10. Mix half the hazelnuts into the chocolate frosting and spread it over the top of the cake. Sprinkle the remaining nuts over the top.

Your cake is now ready for eating.

12 Roast It

ROASTING traditionally meant cooking over a fire, usually on a spit to turn the meat so that it cooked evenly. Roasting in an oven is actually baking. But "baked beef and Yorkshire pudding" doesn't sound quite right, so we still call whole, baked poultry and meats, "roasts". The term "baked" is reserved for fish, bread, vegetables and fruit. There are exceptions such as a whole, baked ham or roast potatoes. Roasting is considered to be a particularly British skill. (See Global Food - Britain.)

A MEAT-EATER'S GUIDE

BEEF - As with all meat, cheap cuts are better cooked long and slow to extract the flavour and make the meat tender. More expensive, prime cuts such as rump steaks need only to be cooked quickly and lightly. The steak should be "marbled" with streaks of fat. The fat of best beef should be creamy-white, firm and brittle.

LAMB - Spring lamb is considered to be of the best quality. Shoulder of lamb is cheaper than leg of lamb. It's fattier but has a sweeter taste. Lamb chops can be cooked quickly under the grill.

PORK - A tender white meat that can be roasted, grilled or used in stews. Roasted pork skin makes crispy crackling. Pork must always be cooked thoroughly for safety. It's very nutritious and higher in B vitamins than other meat. As with most meat, it has more flavour when cooked on the bone.

POULTRY - Fresh is far superior to frozen and free-range is best of all. Cook thoroughly to remove any risk of poisoning.

FOOD POISONING ALERT

It is very important that poultry and pork are completely cooked all the way through. They should never be eaten when pink as this could cause food poisoning (salmonella from chicken and parasites in pork). If you find yourself at the table carving the chicken or pork and discover that it is still pink on the inside, you really must put it back in the oven for more cooking. Of course this poses a problem because your vegetables are ready, the gravy is hot and the guests hungry. But there's nothing worse than poisoning your friends or yourself, so don't take risks.

ROAST CHICKEN WITH APPLE GRAVY, ROAST VEGETABLES AND BREAD SAUCE

This is a perfect meal, energy-efficient, simple to make and very tasty. The chicken, apple, gravy and vegetables are all cooked in the same oven for the same amount of time and at the same temperature. The bread sauce is optional, cooked on the stove, but is well worth the small amount of effort needed to make it.

Preparing the chicken:

Chickens bought from supermarkets are already prepared for roasting. Always check that there are no giblets in the inner cavity. If there are, remove and store them in the freezer to be used later for stock-making (though the liver should not be used for stock). If you prefer to buy your chicken from the butcher, ask him to prepare it for roasting and to put the giblets in a separate bag for freezing.

SERVES FOUR

1 medium size roasting chicken (about 1.35-1.85 kg or 3-4 lbs)
600 ml (1 pt) pure apple juice
2 cloves garlic, peeled and slightly crushed under a wooden spoon
2 teaspoons sunflower oil

Preheat oven to 190°C/375°F/gas mark 5.

1. Wash the chicken inside and out and pat dry with a paper towel.
2. Put the partly crushed garlic inside the chicken cavity.
3. Rub a little oil all over the skin of the chicken.
4. Place the chicken, breast side up, on to a wire rack in a roasting pan. (As a rule the roasting pan should be only slightly larger than the chicken, in order to catch all the juices, but not too big, or the juices will burn.)
5. Pour the apple juice into the roasting pan and carefully place in the preheated oven. This is when you should put your vegetables in. (See next recipes.)
6. Cook the chicken for 20 mins per pound plus 20 mins more.
7. After this time, place a heat-proof mat on a surface as near to your oven as possible. Then, using oven gloves, carefully remove the roasting pan with the cooked chicken from the oven and place it on to the mat. The pan is very hot and heavy so be careful not to burn yourself or drop your chicken!

8. To test that the chicken is fully cooked, stick a skewer or fork into the thigh part of the chicken, above the leg. The chicken is cooked when the liquid comes out clear not pink. If the liquid is still pink, the chicken needs to be returned to the oven for further cooking. Cook for another 10 mins and then repeat the test until the juices run clear.
9. Serve the chicken on a large, preheated plate. Reheat the apple-juice gravy from the roasting pan in a small saucepan and serve it in a jug.

Note:
Roasting chicken usually requires some basting, a technique in which the juices are spooned over the meat during cooking to keep it moist. In this recipe, no basting is needed because the apple juice prevents the chicken from drying out.

Roast Vegetables: Potatoes, Parsnips and Carrots

Crispy roast potatoes, sweet parsnips and carrots complete the delicious roast dinner above. Or have them on their own with the bread sauce as a change from chips and mayonnaise!

SERVES FOUR

3 tablespoons sunflower oil
900 g (2 lb) potatoes
900 g (2 lb) parsnips
225 g (½ lb) carrots

1. **Put the sunflower oil into a roasting pan and place in the oven.**
2. **Peel the potatoes and chop into thirds or halves depending on their size.**
3. **Top and tail the parsnips and cut into chunks of about the same size as the potato chunks. Top and tail the carrots and leave whole.**
4. **Boil the potatoes in a saucepan of water for 3 mins only, drain and leave to dry. This is called "parboiling" because the food is only partially cooked before roasting.**
5. **Put the potatoes and parsnips into the hot roasting pan. Using a spoon, cover the vegetables with the oil and cook in the oven below the chicken, for the same length of time as the chicken (about 1½ hrs). Half way through the cooking, turn the vegetables over to brown on all sides.**
6. **Serve with the roast chicken.**

Bread Sauce

Using bread as a basis for a sauce is another traditional method of making sauces. This is a classic sauce to serve with roast chicken or turkey.
We adore bread sauce so we've made a larger quantity than is usual. If you don't want so much, just use ½ pt milk and 2 oz breadcrumbs.

600 ml (1 pt) milk
1 onion, studded with 3 cloves
8 black peppercorns
1 bay leaf
pinch of nutmeg
110 g (4 oz) fresh white bread, crumbled roughly
30 g (1 oz) butter

1. **Put the onion, peppercorns, bay leaf and nutmeg into a small saucepan with the milk and simmer gently over a low heat for 30 mins to release the flavours into the milk.**
2. **Strain the milk into a bowl and add the breadcrumbs. Allow mixture to stand for 15 mins to release the flavours into the breadcrumbs.**
3. **Add the butter, return to the saucepan and heat the sauce until the butter has melted, stirring occasionally.**
4. **Add salt and pepper to taste.**

13
Steam It

STEAMING is a method of cooking food in steam, the hot vapour produced by boiling liquid, usually water. It's a traditional way to cook puddings and an excellent method of cooking vegetables.

ROBERT'S VEGETABLES

When I was a kid, my parents would never let me leave the table until I'd eaten all my green vegetables. War would break out. I would stubbornly refuse. My parents would insist. After about half an hour, a grumpy compromise would be reached. Like so many children, I came to regard green vegetables as the enemy - floppy and foul, partly because they were always cooked to death. It took me years to discover just how good vegetables can taste.

Judging from the results of our *Eat Up* food survey, the majority of young people avoid vegetables, as I did. We hope we can change your minds and entice you to "eat your greens" by showing you how to make them crisp and tasty. Even that most hated vegetable of all - the cabbage.

Over the last twenty years, the varieties of vegetables available have increased dramatically and we have discovered ways of cooking them so that they look and taste wonderful: oriental stir-fries containing mangetout, bean sprouts, baby corns and carrots; Mediterranean ratatouille with aubergines, courgettes and different coloured bell peppers; fresh salads combining so many shapes, tastes and textures of leaves reflecting all hues of green, and sometimes topped with edible flowers like nasturtiums and pansies. A far cry from my sad salad days!

Steamed Spinach

When you boil green vegetables like spinach, most of the nutrients leaked out into the water are thrown away. So it's much better to steam them. Use a steamer if you have one, or steam in a saucepan with a tight-fitting lid, as in the next recipe.

STEAMED SPINACH

PER PERSON

225 g (½ lb) fresh green spinach

1. **Wash the spinach very carefully several times to remove any grit. Remove any tough stalks. Do not dry but place in a saucepan with a little salt.**
2. **Cover the pan and cook over a low heat for about 3-5 mins until the spinach has shrunk down and is tender.**
3. **Serve at once with a little butter or olive oil and a dash of lemon juice.**

Leeks, courgettes, peas, beans, sweetcorn and other vegetables can be successfully steamed.
LEEKS: Cut into 5 cm (2 in) rounds, wash well and steam in a pan with just enough water to cover the bottom.
COURGETTES: Cut in half lengthways and steam in a little water, as above.
FRENCH GREEN BEANS or MANGETOUT: Top and tail and steam in a little water until tender.

Microwaved Veggies

We've included just this one microwave recipe because this is where these ovens come into their own. Vegetables cooked in a microwave retain their colour and nutrients.

To microwave 450 g (1 lb) courgettes: wash and cut into quarters lengthways. Place in a covered shallow microwave dish and cook for 10-12 mins on full power (650W).

TO PEEL OR NOT TO PEEL?

The most nutritious part of root vegetables like carrots and potatoes is just below the skin. When you peel them, you lose these nutrients. So we usually prefer not to peel vegetables but to scrub them and cook them in their skins.

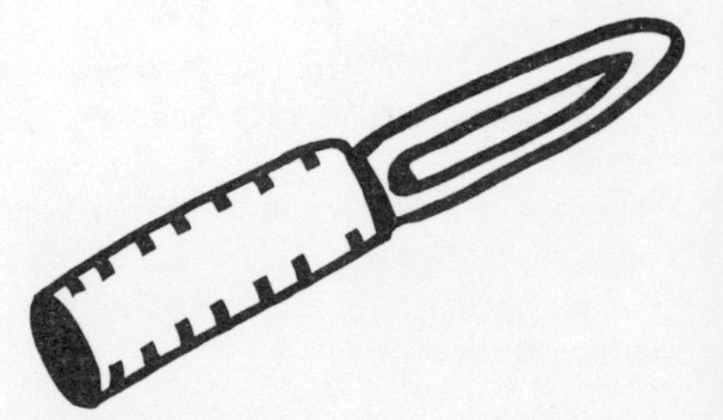

14 Stew It

STEWING is simmering food slowly in liquid in a covered pan over a low heat. This is a delectable way of using cheaper cuts of meat and a variety of vegetables.

PISTO (Vegetable Stew)

A medley of Mediterranean vegetables, Pisto is perfect as a meal in itself for lunch served with brown bread.

PISTO

SERVES TWO

4 tablespoons olive oil
2 onions, chopped
225 g (½ lb) courgettes, sliced, then quartered
2 green or red bell peppers, seeded and chopped
1 teaspoon salt
3 tablespoons passata (sieved tomatoes sold in a bottle or a carton)
1 teaspoon sugar
1 egg, lightly beaten

1. Heat the oil in a large, heavy frying pan until hot.
2. Add the onions, courgettes, peppers and salt. Stir, turn the heat to low, cover and cook for 40 mins, stirring occasionally.
3. Add the passata and sugar and stir. Remove from the heat, pour in the egg, stirring constantly. Serve immediately.

This recipe has no seasoning apart from salt, so try experimenting by adding a herb such as thyme, parsley, coriander or basil when you add the vegetables. See what difference it makes.

IRISH STEW

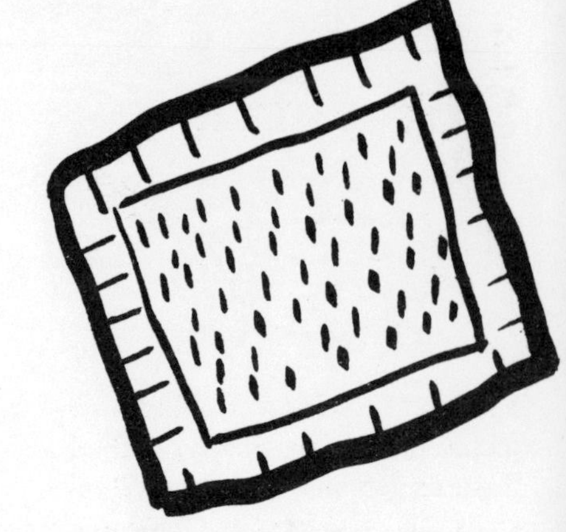

SERVES FOUR

1.35 kg (3 lb) neck of lamb, cut into chunks
1.35 kg (3 lb) potatoes
450 g (1 lb) onions
600 ml (1 pt) water
1 teaspoon dried thyme
1 bouquet garni
salt
pepper

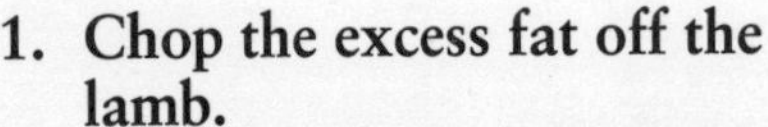

1. Chop the excess fat off the lamb.
2. Scrub the potatoes and slice.
3. Peel the onions and chop into $\frac{1}{4}$ in slices.
4. In a large saucepan, place a layer of potatoes, followed by a layer of onions, followed by a layer of meat. Season with salt and pepper. Continue the layers, ending with a layer of potatoes.
5. Add 1 pint of water, thyme and the bouquet garni.
6. Bring to the boil then simmer, covered, on a low heat for $2\frac{1}{2}$ hrs.

Serve with bread.

15
Stir-fry It

STIR-FRYING is a cooking technique that originated in the Far East, particularly in China. Bite-sized pieces of food are fried in a little oil over a very high flame and stirred frequently. The food is cooked very quickly in a large, round saucepan called a wok. Stir-frying preserves the flavour, texture and nutrients of the food.

Chinese food has its own special seasonings including soy sauce, ginger, garlic and sesame oil. It's great fun to cook and once you've chopped all the ingredients - get your friends to help - it's a very fast way of making a meal. More stir-fried recipes appear in Global Food - China.

A TASTE OF THE ORIENT

SOY SAUCE is made from fermented soy beans and brine. Dark soy sauce is enriched with caramel or molasses. Used extensively in Asian cooking.

GINGER is a root with a pungent, penetrating flavour. You can buy fresh root ginger or dried, ground ginger. The Chinese use chopped ginger root in many dishes.

SESAME OIL has a toasted, nutty flavour and is usually added towards the end of cooking.

All are available in big supermarkets or from Asian shops.

SUPERFLAVOUR

A marinade is a liquid or paste highly seasoned with herbs and spices in which food is soaked (marinated) before cooking. Marinades give food extra flavour, prevent them from drying out and also have a tenderising effect.

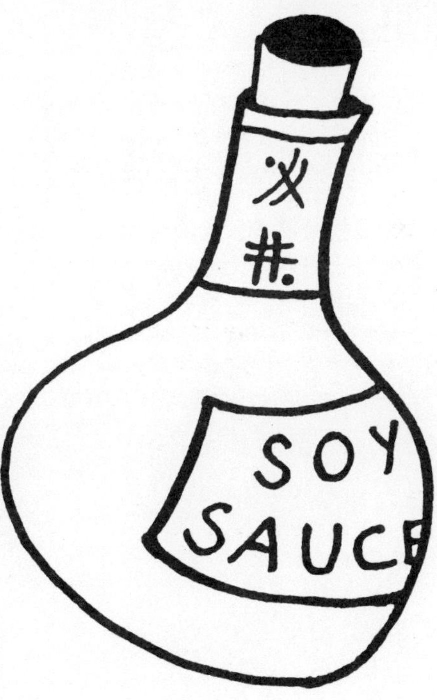

Phil's Beef and Cabbage Stir-fry

Our friend Phil has lived on this since leaving home. It was the only meal he could cook at the time and he's still alive and kicking! If you don't eat meat, the variation using tofu is just as good.

PHIL'S BEEF AND CABBAGE STIR-FRY

SERVES FOUR

MARINADE
2 tablespoons soy sauce
2 tablespoons wine vinegar
2 teaspoons brown sugar

INGREDIENTS
225 g (8 oz) minced beef
350 g (12 oz) white cabbage, shredded
1 onion, sliced
2 cloves garlic, peeled and finely chopped
1 in root ginger, finely chopped
1 tablespoon soy sauce
black pepper
3 tablespoons peanut oil
½ teaspoon chilli oil (optional)

1. Mix the minced beef with the marinade and leave for half an hour.
2. Heat the oil in a wok or heavy, large frying pan until very hot - a small piece of garlic should sizzle at once when dropped in the oil.
3. Add the beef with its marinade to the hot oil. Using a Chinese metal spatula or wooden spoon, stir-fry by stirring and turning the beef constantly until the beef is almost dry (about 5 mins).
4. Add the onion, ginger and garlic and stir-fry for another minute.
5. Add the cabbage with the pepper and stir-fry for 4 mins more.
6. Remove from the heat and stir in 1 tablespoon of soy sauce.
7. Serve with boiled rice.

This recipe might well change your mind about cabbage. It's truly addictive!

VARIATION

This dish works well using tofu (bean curd) instead of meat. Chop the tofu into small cubes and marinate as above. Stage 3 should only take about 3 mins.

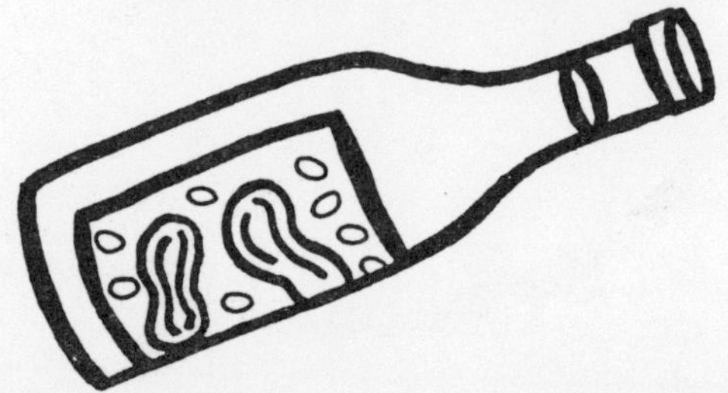

RICE IS NICE

Rice is one of the oldest cultivated crops and today there are over seven thousand different varieties. We can divide them into two main groups:

1. *Long grain:* widely available and includes Basmati rice, commonly used in Indian cookery, which is more expensive and slightly thinner than other long grain rice.

2. *Short grain:* used in puddings. Italian Arborio short grain rice is used in the savoury dish, risotto.

Rice can be either white or brown. Brown rice has the husks left on, adding a delicious nutty flavour. It also retains valuable B vitamins and other nutrients. It takes longer to cook than white rice. Wild rice is the seed of wild grass grown in North America and China. Try it for a treat. Its thin seeds are almost black. Unfortunately wild rice is wildly expensive.

Rice is the only cereal that is exclusively eaten by humans and is not fed to animals.

RICE

Rice goes with almost anything but especially with Chinese stir-fries and Asian curries. It's the staple food of most of Asia where it may be eaten at every meal. The Chinese say that every grain of rice represents a bead of sweat on a peasant's brow. In some parts of Asia, rice is a symbol of life and fertility. This is where we get our custom of throwing rice for luck at weddings.

FOOLPROOF RICE

You can cook rice in many different ways. Here's one that we find works well every time to produce light, fluffy rice.

When you first use this method of rice cooking you will want to check that you have added enough water. The amount of water needed will vary slightly depending on where the long grain rice is from, how old it is, etc. Once you get used to this method and to your rice, you won't need to check and your rice will be perfect every time.

FOOLPROOF RICE

SERVES FOUR TO SIX

380 g (13 oz) long grain white rice
water

pan with a tight-fitting lid
aluminium foil, cut to a size bigger than the saucepan lid

1. Put the rice in a heavy saucepan and wash in several rinses of cold water until rinsing water is clear. This removes some of the starch, making the rice fluffy.
2. Add cold water to cover rice. A good test is to place your hand flat on top of the rice, then add water until it just covers the knuckles on your hand. If in doubt, it's better to add a little less water as you can always add more later.
3. Bring the rice to the boil over a high heat in an uncovered pan.
4. As soon as the rice begins to boil fiercely, place the tin foil over it and the lid on top of the foil. Turn the heat down to as low as possible and leave, covered, to cook for 14 mins. The tin foil helps to seal the pot and stops the steam from escaping.
5. The rice can be served immediately or left to stay warm in the covered pan. Don't take the lid or foil off until it is time to serve. The rice should be light and fluffy, a little chewy and dry. It shouldn't be soggy or chalky. If you are lucky, a layer of crispy rice will form at the bottom of the pan. The crispy rice is considered a great treat in China.

TO CHECK: 10 mins into the cooking time check that the rice has enough water. Quickly take the lid and tin foil off and fluff the rice up with a spoon. The rice should look wet but you shouldn't be able to see any water. If the rice looks dry, add a little more cold water, no more than 3 tablespoons. Stir once, quickly put the foil and lid back on, and cook for 5 more mins.

16
Deep Fry It

DEEP FRYING is frying food by immersing it in very hot oil. The food is either fried plain or coated with a batter or breadcrumbs.

Deep frying has got itself a bad name: soggy, greasy chips and the dangerous chip-pan fire. You can avoid these by following the guidelines in this section.

Deep frying should be easy and safe. Perfectly cooked chips or fritters are light and fluffy on the inside and wonderfully dry and crispy on the outside. The key to successful deep frying is to heat the oil to exactly the right temperature and to keep it at this temperature while frying. The longer a food is fried for, the more oil it absorbs. So if the oil is too cold, the food takes longer to cook, absorbs more oil and will be greasy. If the oil is too hot, the outside will burn and the inside will be undercooked.

The best oil for deep frying is one that heats to a very high temperature without burning. Peanut or ground-nut oil is excellent and corn oil is also good.

You should always use a large, heavy pan with a tight-fitting lid in case you need to put out a fire. (See Fire box on next page.) Only fill your pan **half** full with oil. This leaves plenty of room for the oil to bubble up when the food is added and stops you getting burnt if the oil starts to spit. The food to be fried should be at room temperature. Food straight from the fridge will cause the oil temperature to plummet.

Most deep frying is done at 190°C/375°F. If you do not have a cookery thermometer use the bread test instead: drop a one inch cube of bread into the hot oil. When the oil is the right temperature, it will turn golden brown in 40 secs.

Don't put too much into the pan all at once or the temperature will fall too much. Fry the food in small batches. After each frying, allow a little time for the oil to come back to the correct temperature. Skim off all left-over bits after each frying or else they will burn and flavour the oil. After frying, drain the food well on kitchen paper to remove any excess oil.

Chip-pan fires do happen. Oil is highly flammable and can easily catch fire. We suggest that younger people should make sure a responsible adult is nearby before they start deep frying. And you must never leave your chip pan unattended for a moment when cooking.

If a fire does start *DO NOT PANIC.* Quickly get the adult to turn off the heat and put the lid on the pan. This cuts off the oxygen and puts out the fire. If you are using a pan without a lid (not recommended) keep a damp tea towel nearby just in case. If a fire starts, cover the pan with the damp cloth to put it out. Make sure you put the cloth down away from you, otherwise the flames will be wafted into your face. Here are some more crucial rules:

1. Never pour water on the fire. This makes it spread.

2. Never move a burning pan. You could spill it, setting fire to yourself and the kitchen.

My grandmother's cousin died from burns when he carried a chip fire out of the back door. As he opened the door, the wind blew the fire towards him setting him on fire.

CHIPS

SERVES FOUR

900 g (2 lb) old potatoes

1. Peel the potatoes, cut into slices, then cut the slices into strips (0.5-1 cm (¼-½in) wide or any size you want.
2. Soak in cold water for 15 mins or so.
3. Drain and dry thoroughly.
4. When the oil has reached the required temperature (see page 75) carefully drop in the chips and fry for about 6 mins until they are soft and turning golden.
5. Remove the chips from the pan and drain well on kitchen towel.
6. When the oil has again reached the required temperature, fry the same chips for a second time for 1-2 mins, until crisp and golden.
7. Drain again on kitchen towel and serve.

17
Batter It

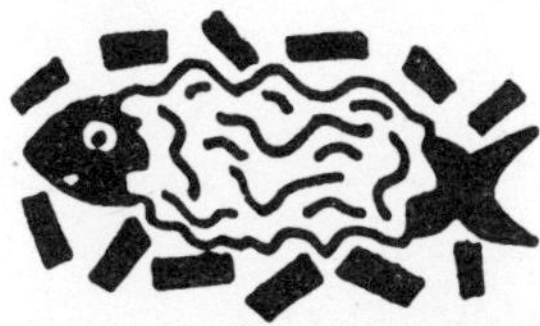

Many foods that are deep fried are first coated in batter. (Examples of this can be found in the Global Food section: e.g. fish and chips on page 99.) Batter is a mixture of flour and liquid, usually with eggs added.

Remember, you don't have to wait for Pancake Day to enjoy sweet or savoury pancakes!

PANCAKES

SERVES FOUR

110 g (4 oz) plain flour
pinch of salt
1 egg
1 egg yolk
1 tablespoon sunflower oil
300 ml (½ pt) milk

1. **Make the batter. First put the flour and salt in a large bowl, make a well in the centre, drop in the egg and egg yolk and a little of the milk and beat to a smooth paste.**
2. **Gradually add the rest of the milk, stirring continuously until you have a smooth batter.**
3. **Place in the fridge for 30 mins.**
4. **Heat a frying pan over a medium heat, add a few drops of oil and spread around with a spatula.**
5. **Add 2 tablespoons of batter to the pan, tilt it round and round so the batter covers most of the pan.**
6. **After 2-3 mins, edge the spatula under the pancake and flip it over. Leave for 10 secs then remove to a plate. Repeat, adding a drop of oil to the pan occasionally. Stack the pancakes and keep them warm.**

PANCAKE FILLINGS

For a British version of the famous French pancakes called crêpes Suzettes simply fill your pancake with some lemon juice and caster sugar, roll up and devour!

For savoury pancakes, fill with the same toppings as for baked potatoes such as chopped ham, grated cheese or fresh herbs. Or invent your own!

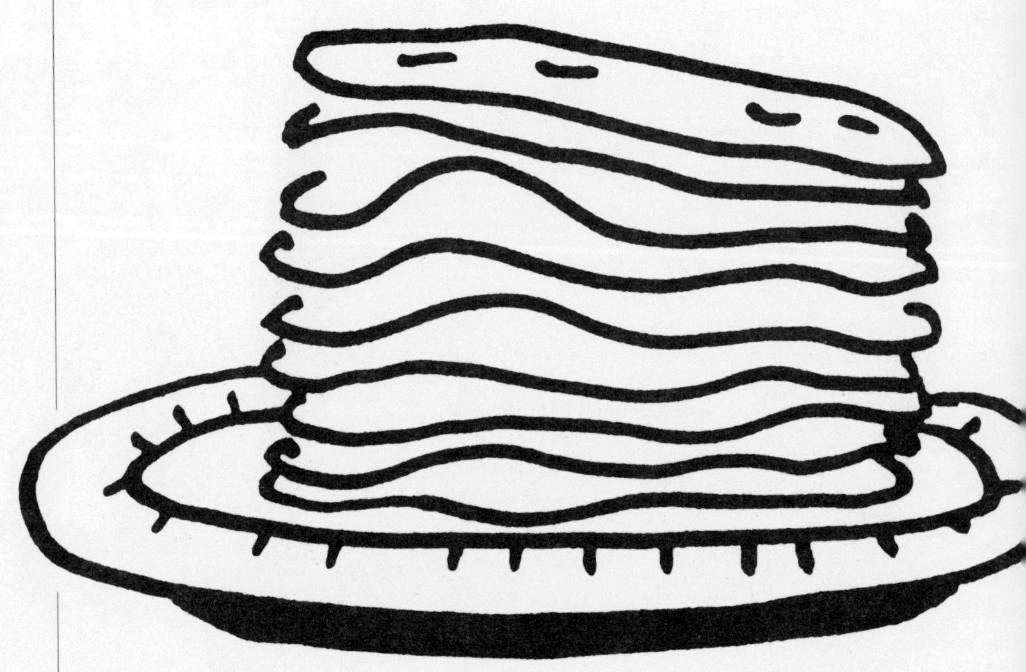

PART TWO
Global Food

18
AFRICA

Africa is a huge continent of many different countries and cooking styles. In many parts of Africa, a standard meal consists of two main elements: vegetables such as the starchy cassava root, plantains (similar to bananas), yams and sweet potatoes which form the basis of many sweet and savoury dishes and are cooked in lots of different ways; and cereal grains such as corn, rice, sorghum or millet which are the other source of carbohydrates in the diet. Stews and soups containing meat, fish, pulses and nuts provide the protein and flavour, boosted by hot chillies and, depending on the region's climate, palm oil and coconut milk.

When I was sixteen, I was lucky enough to visit the amazing island of Madagascar, off the east coast of Africa. I tasted some of the best seafood and tropical fruit I've ever eaten at Madame Dubois' cafe on the beach at Morondava.

The Arabs, the Portuguese and the Dutch, as well as British colonial influences from India, have all left their mark on African cooking. African food itself has travelled across the world mainly to South America, the Caribbean and the southern states of America like Louisiana. The extraordinary vegetable okra (known as "lady's fingers" in America, because of its shape) is called "gumbo" in parts of Africa. Many shops and markets in this country now stock delicious sweet potatoes and yams. Try them instead of potatoes or rice.

The first two simple recipes in this section are from Ghana, in West Africa, where peanuts are a staple source of protein. The peanut stew contains chicken and the other is a tasty mixture of vegetables. They may sound unusual combinations but do give them a try. We love them. The third recipe is a wonderful couscous, a classic North African dish made with lamb, the favoured meat of the Muslim people.

PEANUT STEW

Very simple and economical to make. The ingredients combine to give a fantastic flavour and a wonderful texture. Try it once and you'll be hooked!

PEANUT STEW

SERVES SIX

1.8 kg (4 lb) chicken, skinned and cut into 8 pieces
2 onions, chopped
400 g (14 oz) can chopped tomatoes
110 g (4 oz) peanut butter, unsweetened
225 g (8 oz) okra, topped and tailed
1 small can (215 g) butter beans, drained

1. Put the onion and chicken in a pot (without oil) and brown slightly.
2. Cover with water, bring to the boil and skim the chicken fat from the surface.
3. Mash the butter beans and tomatoes with a fork, add to the stew and simmer for 45 mins.
4. Put the peanut butter in a bowl, add some liquid from the pot and mix until smooth and runny.
5. Return to the pot and continue to simmer for another 15 mins.
6. Add the okra and simmer for 15 mins.

Serve with rice.

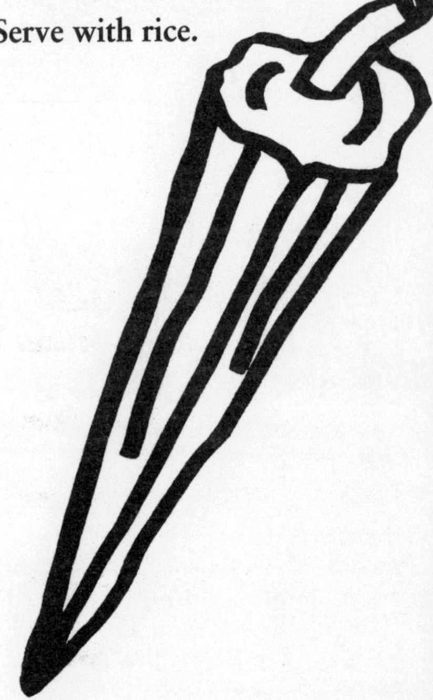

OKRA

Okra is a tropical plant, "gumbo" in Africa. It is widely grown as a vegetable crop and is rich in iron, calcium and vitamin C. When cooked, okra releases a kind of gooey juice; it sounds disgusting but is excellent for thickening soups. Okra was introduced to North America by the African slaves brought over to work on the plantations. It is widely used in Cajun and Creole cooking, (see page 89).

MAFE

Every ladleful of this wonderful stew is packed with different vegetables. It's like playing lucky dip: you never know what you are going to get next.

MAFE

SERVES EIGHT

4 tablespoons olive oil
450 g (1 lb) onions, finely chopped
2 fresh green chillies, finely chopped
3 cloves garlic, peeled and minced
225 g (8 oz) potatoes, cut into large chunks
3 small turnips, cut into large chunks
225 g (8 oz) carrots, sliced
450 g (1 lb) pumpkin, cut into large chunks
450 g (1 lb) sweet potatoes, cut into large chunks
600 ml (1 pt) water
2 tablespoons tomato purée
400 g (14 oz) tin tomatoes
450 g (1 lb) mixed greens (cabbage, spinach etc.)
110 g (4 oz) peanut butter (without added sugar)
salt and pepper

1. Heat the oil in a stew pot then sauté the onions over a medium heat until soft.
2. Add the chillies and garlic and cook for a few more minutes.
3. Add the potatoes and turnips and cook for a further 15 mins.
4. Add the carrots, pumpkin and sweet potatoes and cook for 10 mins.
5. Mix the water with the tomato purée and add to the pot together with the tomatoes.
6. Bring to the boil and then simmer slowly until the vegetables are nearly cooked.
7. Finally, add the greens and then the peanut butter, mixed with a cup of the broth to make it smooth and runny.
8. Stir and simmer for 15 mins. Add salt and pepper to taste.

Serve with boiled rice.

VARIATIONS

If you are lucky enough to live near a shop where you can buy yams and plantains, add them too. Peel the yams and chop to the size of the other vegetables. Peel the plantain and cut into quarters. Swedes and aubergines also go well in this stew.

LAMB COUSCOUS

This recipe is from Francis Boukraa and her husband Abdel, who comes from Tunisia. They run Adams Café in West London which serves British food by day and traditional Tunisian food at night. This is one of their most popular dishes. You may have seen them cooking it on Channel 4's *Food File* programmes.

This recipe benefits from the use of cheaper cuts of meat. (You can also make it with chicken or just vegetables.) It's a great party dish and very economical. The recipe below serves six people and costs less than a pound a head.

LAMB COUSCOUS

SERVES SIX

3 tablespoons tomato purée
2 teaspoons paprika
1 teaspoon each turmeric and black pepper
½ teaspoon each cumin, coriander, ginger and salt
1 onion, chopped
3 carrots, diced
2 turnips, diced
4 courgettes, sliced
2 large potatoes, chopped
2 tomatoes, chopped
400 g (14 oz) can chick peas, drained
2 cloves garlic, peeled and chopped
8 tablespoons olive oil
450 g (1 lb) lamb (neck or shoulder), cut into chunks
450 g (1 lb) couscous
600 ml (1 pt) water
harissa (if available) or any other chilli sauce (to serve at the table so your guests can make the couscous as hot as they want)

COUSCOUS

An African cereal made from hard, durum wheat semolina rubbed between dampened hands to form tiny balls the size of poppy seeds. It is a staple food throughout the Middle East and Africa.

Garnish: 2 sliced, hard boiled eggs, a few black olives or sultanas

1. Pour the olive oil into a large, heavy saucepan and heat.
2. Put the onion and the garlic into the oil and sauté until golden.
3. Pour in the tomato purée and the meat with 100 ml of the water and season with salt, pepper, turmeric, paprika, cumin, coriander and ginger and stir.
4. Pour in half a litre of water, bring to the boil, cover and simmer over a low heat for 30 mins.
5. Add the chopped carrots, chopped potatoes, chopped turnips and simmer for 30 mins.
6. Add the courgettes, chopped tomatoes and drained, tinned chick peas to the stew and simmer for 30 mins.
7. Prepare the couscous grains as directed on the packet.

Once cooked, put the couscous in a large bowl, pour the stew over it and serve garnished with sliced, hard boiled eggs, olives or sultanas. Enjoy your party!

VARIATIONS

1. For the vegetarian alternative, substitute the meat with white cabbage, swedes, pumpkins and broad beans or vegetables of your choice.
2. If you want to use dried chick peas, first soak them overnight in water, drain and add to the stew at stage 5, with the water.
3. If you have a large steamer (or even a couscousier - the real thing!) cook your stew in the bottom and steam the couscous grains on top.

19
America

We often think of American food as being traditionally based on English cooking, but there's a lot more to it than that. Native American Indian, French, German, Italian, Irish, Chinese, Mexican - all these, along with other ethnic and religious groups such as Jewish, Cajun and Creole, make American food a fascinating melting pot of tastes and cuisines.

The Americans have popularised many of their culinary talents in the form of fast food outlets: the hamburger, southern-fried chicken, the hot dog. You've already made one of their famous snack foods for your first recipe - popcorn! They also invented the ice-cream cone and crisps. It's said that crisps or potato chips were invented when a customer kept on complaining to the chef that his french fries were not thin enough. So, in a rage, the chef sliced the potatoes wafer-thin and deep fried them. The crisp was born!

HAMBURGERS

Hamburgers do not take their name from their meat content but from the German city of Hamburg. It was the Germans who first brought the hamburger to North America. This style of preparing beef came originally from the Russians who in turn adapted it from the Tartars. The Tartars were a tribe of people who liked to eat raw, ground beef. ("Steak tartare" is the name given to a dish of raw, ground beef still eaten today.)

The Americans' great invention was to put the hamburger in the bun. Hamburgers' immense popularity started back in the 1920s and today they are one of America's most famous exports, with hamburger bars in all the major cities of the world - a mixed blessing, perhaps.

Hamburgers made at home, whether in the kitchen or on a barbecue, are an all-time favourite with meat-eaters. They are easy and fun to make. It's best to use good quality meat, like lean mince or ground rump steak, for flavour and texture.

HAMBURGERS

MAKES FOUR HAMBURGERS

450 g (1 lb) lean mince, finely ground
1 onion, grated
1 teaspoon Worcestershire sauce
1 teaspoon ground black pepper
salt
4 hamburger buns

1. Mix all the ingredients thoroughly together in a bowl and shape into 4 patties as big as the buns you are going to use.
2. Put a few grains of salt in a frying pan and heat over a medium heat.
3. Dry fry hamburgers for 7 mins on each side.

Choose your own hamburger relish. Try the sauce from the spareribs in the recipe below, together with sliced dill pickles, sliced raw onions and grated cheese.

OVEN-BARBECUED SPARERIBS

These spare ribs really are "finger-lickin' good" !

OVEN-BARBECUED SPARERIBS

SERVES FOUR OR MORE

900 g (2 lb) spareribs

FOR SAUCE
140 g (5 oz) granulated brown sugar
2 teaspoons dry mustard
1 teaspoon salt
½ teaspoon black pepper
1.5cm (½in) fresh ginger, chopped finely, or
½ teaspoon ground ginger
½ teaspoon ground cinnamon
225 ml (8 fl oz) sieved tomatoes (passata)
100 ml (4 fl oz) wine vinegar
1 teaspoon Tabasco sauce
1 small onion, grated
1 clove garlic, peeled and crushed

Preheat oven to 180°C/350°F/gas mark 4.

1. Place the spareribs on a rack over a shallow pan and roast for 45 mins.
2. Meanwhile, combine the sugar and spices in a saucepan.
3. Add the remaining ingredients and bring to the boil over a medium heat, stirring occasionally, for 5 mins.
4. Pour a third of the sauce over the spareribs and continue to roast for 30 mins.
5. Turn the ribs and pour half the remaining sauce over them.
6. Roast for 1 hour, brushing with the extra sauce several times during this period.

Texan Chilli con Carne

This recipe is a favourite of students Richard, Josh and Philip, who let us film them making this chilli for the Eat Up television series. It's a famous Texan dish perfect for parties or feeding any crowd. People argue endlessly about how you should make it: chunks of meat or mince? Fresh chillies or chilli powder? Beans and tomatoes?

What does it matter when it tastes this good?

TEXAN CHILLI CON CARNE

SERVES FOUR

2 green bell peppers, finely chopped
225 g (½ lb) onions, peeled and finely chopped
2 cloves garlic, peeled and finely chopped
4 dried hot little red chillies
2 tablespoons sunflower oil
675 g (1½lb) lean minced beef
½ teaspoon ground cumin
½ teaspoon dried oregano
1 bay leaf
400 g (14 oz) can plum tomatoes
400 g (14 oz) can red kidney beans, drained and rinsed
1 teaspoon sugar

1. Soak the dried chilli peppers in just enough water to cover, for 30 mins. Then chop finely and keep the soaking water.
2. Heat the oil in a heavy saucepan or frying pan and add the minced beef, bell peppers, onions and garlic. Sauté over a low/medium heat, stirring occasionally, until the meat is lightly

browned all over. Break up any large lumps of meat while stirring.

3. Add the chopped chillies, cumin, oregano, bay leaf, tomato and chilli water.
4. Bring to the boil, turn the heat to low and simmer with the lid on for 1½ hrs.
5. Add the red kidney beans 30 mins before the end of the cooking time.

Serve with cornbread or rice.

Cook It Cabbage Salad - Coleslaw

This all-time favourite is thought to originate from the Dutch word 'slaw', meaning cabbage.

COOK IT CABBAGE SALAD – COLESLAW

SERVES FOUR OR MORE

1 medium-sized cabbage, finely sliced
3 carrots, grated
1 green bell pepper, diced
½ apple, grated
½ onion, grated
3 tablespoons olive oil
2 tablespoons white wine vinegar
juice of one small lemon
1 tablespoon strong mustard
1 teaspoon sugar
1 level teaspoon salt
5 tablespoons yoghurt
black pepper

Garnish: sunflower seeds

1. Finely slice the cabbage, cover with cold water and leave for 30 mins. This makes the cabbage nice and crispy.
2. In a small bowl, mix together the olive oil, vinegar, mustard, sugar and salt. To this add the yoghurt, grated onion, apple and diced pepper.
3. When the cabbage is ready, drain it in a colander and dry by placing a plate over the top and shaking off the excess water (or, alternatively, use a lettuce spinner).
4. Grate the carrot and mix this with the dried cabbage shreds and prepared dressing.
5. Put the coleslaw in the fridge and serve chilled, garnished with sunflower seeds.

Some people like to leave the coleslaw for at least 1 hr to allow the flavours to develop.

Potato Salad

This is excellent for summer lunches and barbecues.

POTATO SALAD

SERVES FOUR

900 g (2 lb) small new potatoes
3 tablespoons olive oil
1 tablespoon wine vinegar
1 teaspoon salt
1 teaspoon black pepper
55 g (2 oz) chives, chopped or 3 spring onions, finely chopped

1. Scrub the potatoes and put in a saucepan, cover with water and bring to the boil over a high heat.
2. Turn the heat to low and simmer for 10 mins.
3. Drain the potatoes, chop them into largish, bite-sized chunks and place in a bowl. Add the oil, vinegar, salt and pepper and mix lightly, then leave to cool.
4. Add the chives or spring onions just before serving.

VARIATION

Instead of using oil and vinegar you could substitute 3 tablespoons of mayonnaise and 3 tablespoons of Greek yoghurt.

Cornbread

This cornbread is the colour of the huge American cornfields. Its crumbly texture and slightly sweet taste make it a perfect companion to Chilli con Carne or Baked Beans. In fact we eat it with almost everything!

This recipe works well but, as with all flour recipes, the amount of liquid you need to add can vary depending on the make of flour you use.

CORNBREAD

SERVES FOUR TO SIX with a meal

140 g (5 oz) fine cornmeal
140 g (5 oz) flour (use a mixture of wholemeal and plain)
1½ tablespoons baking powder
1 teaspoon salt
2 tablespoons brown sugar
2 tablespoons sunflower oil
300 ml (½ pt) milk
50-100 ml (2-4 fl oz) water, depending on the flour

Preheat oven to 200°C/400°F/gas mark 6 and heat your oiled 25 x 15 cm (10 x 6 in) baking tin in the oven while you make the batter.

1. Mix all the dry ingredients together in a mixing bowl.
2. Gently whisk in the liquid ingredients and the water bit by bit until the batter is thin and pourable.
3. Pour the batter into the baking tin and cook in the oven for 30 mins or until the bread is brown on top.
4. Remove from the oven, run a knife around the edge of the tin and transfer to a bread board for serving.

Baked Beans

A real winter warmer with enough left over for beans on toast in the morning.

BAKED BEANS

SERVES FOUR

450 g (1 lb) dried beans (haricot, navy, pinto or kidney)
225 g (8 oz) slab streaky bacon
3 tablespoons maple syrup or treacle
1 teaspoon dry mustard
½ teaspoon salt
1 teaspoon pepper

1. Soak the beans overnight in a large bowl filled with water.
2. Drain the beans and place in a large saucepan with fresh water to cover.
3. Bring them to the boil, then cover and simmer over a low heat for 45 mins.
4. Drain the beans, reserving the cooking water.
5. Preheat the oven to 130°C/250°F/gas mark 1-2.
6. Put the bacon in a casserole dish and cover it with the beans.
7. Mix 1 pt of the cooking water with the maple syrup, mustard, salt and pepper and pour this liquid over the beans.
8. Cover the casserole and bake it in the oven for about 6 hrs.

Serve with cornbread and salad.

You can cook this dish in the morning and have it when you return from school or work, in which case you should add half a pint more water to ensure the beans don't dry up.

Cajun Food

Cajun cooking originates from the southern state of Louisiana. The name "Cajun" comes from the word "Acadian". The Acadians were a group of people who left France in the early seventeenth century to settle in Nova Scotia. In 1755 they were driven out by the English and after a long trek eventually settled in Louisiana. Cajun cooking is a mixture of French, native American Indian, Spanish and African cooking styles.

The Cajun people were mostly rural shrimpers and were very poor, but their food was so good that word spread and now Cajun cooking – basic, earthy and rustic – has become popular all over the United States and Europe. Creole cooking, a close neighbour, is a city food, based in New Orleans and more heavily influenced by the thriving black community who live there.

Sonia Allison is a food writer and broadcaster who has written more than fifty cookery books. Her chosen recipes, from her book *Cooking Cajun-Creole*, are fun and easy to make.

Sonia Allison's Cajun Meat Loaf

Sonia describes it as:
"A novelty meat loaf concocted from minced beef and pork sausage meat. It's a good thing to have around, economical, herby, bright as a button and a perfect partner for Creole sauce. In Louisiana, the obvious accompaniment would be rice – here, potatoes perhaps."

SONIA ALLISON'S CAJUN MEAT LOAF

SERVES SIX TO EIGHT

450 g (1 lb) lean minced beef
225 g (8 oz) pork sausage-meat
125 g (4 oz) onions, peeled and grated
75 g (3 oz) celery, well-scrubbed and very finely chopped
65 g (2½ oz) white bread, cubed
125 ml (4 fl oz) hot milk
1 size 1 or 2 egg, beaten
½ teaspoon Tabasco sauce
1 level teaspoon salt
1 level teaspoon dried thyme
1 level teaspoon French mustard

1. Knead together the beef and sausage-meat with dampened hands. Work in the onions and celery.
2. Put the bread into a bowl. Add the milk. Soak for 5 mins then gradually beat in the egg. Work into the meat mixture thoroughly.
3. Fork in the Tabasco sauce, salt, thyme and mustard. Shape into a 20 x 10 cm (8 x 4 in) loaf.
4. Transfer to a piece of greased foil lining a baking tray and cook for 1¼ hrs in an oven set to 180°C/350°F/gas mark 4.
5. Cut the loaf into slices and serve. If there are any left-overs, slice and use in sandwiches or eat cold with salad.

Sonia Allison's Creole Sauce

Sonia writes:
"Hot, hotter, hottest sums up this gutsy sauce which the locals serve as a matter of course with meat loaves, sausages, chicken, game, rice and pasta - even fried fish sometimes. It can easily set you afire, which is why the quantity of Tabasco has been left blank. It's up to you to add as much or as little as you like. (Start with 4 drops only.)"

SONIA ALLISON'S CREOLE SAUCE

SERVES SIX

2 tablespoons oil
125 g (4 oz) onion, peeled and finely chopped
75 g (3 oz) celery, well-scrubbed and finely chopped
125 g (4 oz) washed green pepper, de-seeded and finely chopped
1 clove garlic, peeled and crushed
400 g (14 oz) can tomatoes
1 level teaspoon molasses or molasses sugar
1 tablespoon fresh lemon juice
$^1/_8$ teaspoon ground bay leaves
1 level teaspoon salt
Tabasco sauce to taste

1. **Sizzle the oil in a pan. Add the next 4 ingredients and cook over a moderate heat for about 7-10 mins or until soft and only just beginning to turn golden.**
2. **Add the tomatoes, crushing each one against the sides of the pan.**
3. **Stir in the remaining ingredients, bring slowly to the boil and simmer gently, with the lid on the pan, for 15 mins.**
4. **Stir 2 or 3 times and serve with your main dish.**

Onions, peppers and celery are called 'the Trinity' and form the basis of many Louisiana dishes. They also feature in the next recipe.

Chicken Gumbo

This classic Cajun dish was first cooked for us by Alicia Zervigon, who was brought up in New Orleans. She believes that eating should be a celebration of life and every meal a party! We agree.

Chicken Gumbo is an exotic and economical dish that is perfect for parties or as a family meal. The Cajun spices give it a tantalising and unusual taste.

CHICKEN GUMBO

SERVES SIX

8 tablespoons olive oil
2 green bell peppers, chopped
½ head celery, roughly chopped (including leaves)
450 g (1 lb) onions, sliced
225 g (8 oz) smoked gammon or smoked bacon, cut into chunks
2 chicken quarters
3 cloves garlic, peeled and crushed
450 g (1 lb) okra, topped and tailed and cut in half
2 tablespoons Cajun seasoning (see below)
2 bay leaves
2 teaspoons oregano
salt

1. Pour the olive oil into a large pot and sauté the peppers, celery and onions until soft.
2. Add the meat, garlic, okra, Cajun seasoning, bay leaves and oregano and mix thoroughly.
3. Cover the mixture with water and bring to the boil.
4. Boil for 10 mins, then turn down the heat, cover and simmer for approximately 2½ hrs, adding more water if necessary (remember this is a soup).
5. Towards the end of the cooking time, the chicken should have fallen away from the bones. If not, separate it with a fork and return it, with the bones, to the soup. Add salt to taste.

Serve on top of a little boiled rice.

Cajun Seasoning

If you cannot get any Cajun seasoning, use the following mixture instead:

1 teaspoon salt
1 teaspoon white pepper
1 teaspoon black pepper
1 teaspoon cayenne pepper
1 teaspoon poultry seasoning
1 teaspoon dried basil
1 teaspoon cumin

VARIATION

For a change, or if you don't eat meat, try using pumpkin and root vegetables such as potatoes, carrots and parsnips instead of the meat. Cook for just 1 hr and, 15 mins before the end, add some chopped spinach leaves.

20 BRAZIL

Brazil isn't only famous for its wild carnival. Its cooking is wild too! It has strong Portuguese, Guaraní, Indian and Black African influences. The Portuguese brought the Africans over to work as slaves on their plantations, where the Guaraní Indians introduced cassava to them and thus to Africa.

Rice, beans and cassava are the most important staple foods in the Brazilian diet. In fact, Brazil produces more beans than any other country. Coffee beans are a major export as well as delicious Brazil nuts.

Elisabeth Lambert Ortiz's unusual and scrumptious recipe for Brazilian Chicken with Bananas is from her book, *The Book of Latin American Cooking,* a must for anyone interested in the cooking and history of this region. We've also included some fascinating facts on the banana from Michael Balfour, the author of the soon-to-be-published *BANANAS! The Official Guide.*

Elisabeth Lambert Ortiz's Chicken with Bananas (Frango com Bananas)

Elisabeth writes:
"This chicken dish from Brazil's Mato Grosso is simmered with white wine and tomatoes, then topped with lightly fried bananas. A most attractive and unusual combination of flavours, slightly sweet, slightly sour."

ELISABETH LAMBERT ORTIZ'S CHICKEN WITH BANANAS

SERVES FOUR

1 medium chicken (about 1.4 kg or 3 lb), quartered
4 tablespoons lemon juice
2 teaspoons salt
40 g (1½oz) butter
1 medium onion, grated
2 tomatoes, peeled, seeded and chopped
⅛ teaspoon sugar
300 ml (½) pint dry white wine
4 tablespoons vegetable oil
6 ripe bananas, peeled and halved lengthwise
100 g (4 oz) grated Parmesan cheese
12.5 g (½ oz) butter

1. Season the chicken with the lemon juice and salt.
2. Heat the butter in a flameproof casserole and stir in the onion, tomatoes, and sugar.
3. Add the chicken pieces and any of their liquid. Simmer for 5 mins, uncovered, turning the chicken pieces once.
4. Add the wine, cover the casserole, and simmer until the chicken is tender, about 45 mins.
5. Heat the oil in a pan and sauté the bananas until they are lightly browned on both sides.
6. Arrange the bananas, cut side down, on top of the chicken pieces and sprinkle them with the grated cheese. Dot with the butter, cut into tiny pieces.
7. Place the casserole under the grill for a few mins until the cheese is lightly browned.

Serve with white rice.

Amaze your friends with this new taste sensation.

Michael Balfour's Bananas

Michael Balfour, formally a book publisher, now writes full time on a wide variety of subjects; these include archaeology, wrist-watches, health food - and of course, bananas.

"Bananas are a highly convenient fruit which provide very healthy diet contributions. They come ready-packaged in biodegradable skins, and are easy to eat and digest as tasty quick snacks, desserts or accompaniments. Bananas are great energy boosters before taking exercise or between meals through their readily absorbed sugars.

"Bananas are delicious when incorporated in recipes, and moreover they are also a valuable ingredient. They are rich in carbohydrates; the sugar content increases and their starch decreases as bananas ripen (when 'spotting' appears). They also contain most of the essential vitamins, and are particularly appreciated for their high vitamin C content.

"Among their essential minerals, potassium (good for the nervous system) is richly represented, while sodium is among the lowest. So bananas are ideal for those seeking to avoid fats and salt, and for aids to healing and infection resistance.

"The banana (from the Arabic word '*banan*' which means 'finger') grows mostly in the tropics in over 100 varieties and is popular all over the world. It comes as one of a bunch (or 'hand') and is harvested when still green; the ripening into its familiar yellow state occurs mostly during transportation. Next to the apple the banana is known to be the world's most popular fruit - although in fact it is a giant herb!"

Cook It Latin American Salad

When Columbus stumbled upon the "New World" in 1492 he had no idea what a huge discovery he had made. Not only had he found a new land but also an amazing variety of new foods: potatoes, tomatoes, corn, beans, pumpkins and squashes, sunflowers, peanuts, chocolate, chillies, avocados, pineapples... the list goes on and on.

This recipe celebrates these discoveries.

LATIN AMERICAN SALAD

SERVES TWO TO FOUR

Basic vinaigrette dressing
1 or 2 ripe avocados, should be slightly soft, with no bruising
4 ripe tomatoes
1 oz sweetcorn (canned)
½ oz pumpkin seeds
½ oz sunflower seeds

1. **Cut the avocados in half, remove the stones, peel and slice.**
2. **Slice the tomatoes into rounds.**
3. **Rinse the sweetcorn and drain in a sieve.**
4. **Lay the avocado slices and tomato slices on a serving plate.**
5. **Sprinkle the sweetcorn, pumpkin and sunflower seeds over the top.**
6. **Pour the vinaigrette dressing over this and serve.**

21 BRITAIN

The history of food in Britain really began in the fifth century when invaders came from northern Europe. They settled in the south east of England and slowly cleared away the huge, ancient forests, converting them into what is today called the Garden of England. These northern Europeans brought with them new skills: baking, brewing, cheese-making and butter-churning. They kept livestock and hunted in the forests for deer, wild boar, fruits, berries and mushrooms. During the winter, food was scarce so they had to survive on what they could store from the previous summer's supplies. They preserved the food by drying, smoking or salting, methods still used today.

To mask the bad taste of food that was past its best, spices and herbs were used for flavouring. William the Conqueror and his Norman invaders, who loved good cooking and rich spices, had a lasting effect on our cooking. In the sixteenth century many Dutch fled to Britain, bringing with them root vegetables like carrots and turnips which not only fed the people but kept their animals alive during the winter months. But the British didn't take well to vegetables, and only used them for soups and stews. Fruit was only eaten as a luxury by the rich.

Britain was traditionally a nation of meat-eaters, for those who could afford it. It relied on the quality of its meat, and roasting is still considered a traditionally British art.

Puddings, like black pudding and haggis, are another British speciality, made of minced meat or pigs' blood, cereal and spices. Christmas pudding was originally plum pudding and dated back to the time of Queen Elizabeth the First, when sugar became more affordable. The popularity of sweet puddings meant that "pudding" came to describe not just the dish but also a course at the end of the meal: "What's for pudding?"

The growth of the British Empire meant that people returning from years spent abroad in countries like India brought back a taste for chilli, cumin and other spices. So pickles, chutnies and curries became popular in Britain.

The Second World War also had a dramatic effect on food in Britain. Sugar, butter and many other foods were highly restricted and food-rationing continued into the early fifties. Some say that our diet was healthier then than it is today, without all the sugary, fatty, processed foods we now devour. Ask your gran and see what she says!

We are lucky today that we can buy foods and produce from all over the world. This has allowed us to become much more adventurous in our choice of food. But many foods, particularly fruit and vegetables which used to be grown here, are now flown in from abroad because it's cheaper. This is a pity since part of the fun of fresh food is enjoying the seasonal variations of the country you live in.

Toad in the Hole

A favourite British dish which used to be made with the left-overs from the Sunday roast and Yorkshire pudding. Nowadays the "Toad" is normally a sausage. Vegetarians can replace the sausages with vegetables.

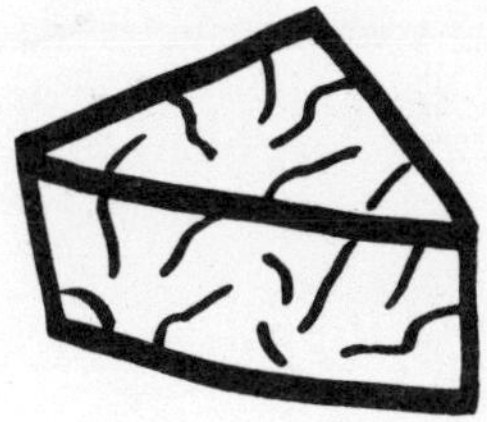

TOAD IN THE HOLE

SERVES FOUR

280 g (10 oz) plain flour
3 eggs
1 teaspoon salt
600 ml (1 pt) milk
black pepper
450 g (1 lb) small pork sausages
2 tablespoons oil

1. Put the flour and salt in a bowl and make a well in the middle.
2. Add the eggs and gradually mix in the flour
3. Add half the milk, stirring continually, until you have a thick, smooth batter.
4. Add the rest of the milk and stir until you have a thin, smooth batter.

BRITISH CHEESES

Cheese is one of the oldest man-made foods, thanks to all the women who worked as dairymaids, milking the cows and churning the butter. It is a rich food, high in protein and fat, and generations of Britons, rich and poor alike, lived on a basic diet of bread and cheese washed down with ale. Queen Victoria was once given a giant Cheddar cheese said to weigh over a thousand pounds.

Cheshire is the oldest of Britain's cheeses although Cheddar is now the most widely eaten. Unfortunately, much of the packaged Cheddar sold in shops has very little flavour. It's worth buying from a good cheese shop if you can. Wensleydale, Caerphilly, Gloucester, Red Leicester and many others each have a distinctive flavour, so try them all.

Britain is famous for its blue cheeses like Stilton. The blue fungus that gives it its colour is the same as the mould you find on old bread. The blueing of a cheese completely changes its taste and texture. One of our favourite blue cheeses is Blue Shropshire.

5. Leave for 30 mins.
6. Preheat the oven to 200°C/400°F/gas mark 6. Put the oil and the sausages in a roasting pan and place in the oven for 10-15 mins until the fat is hot and the sausages brown.
7. Add the batter to the roasting pan.
8. Bake in the middle of the preheated oven for 30-35 mins, until the Yorkshire pudding has risen and is brown on top.

VARIATION
An over-the-top addition is to put cooked bacon as well as sausages in your Toad in the Hole.

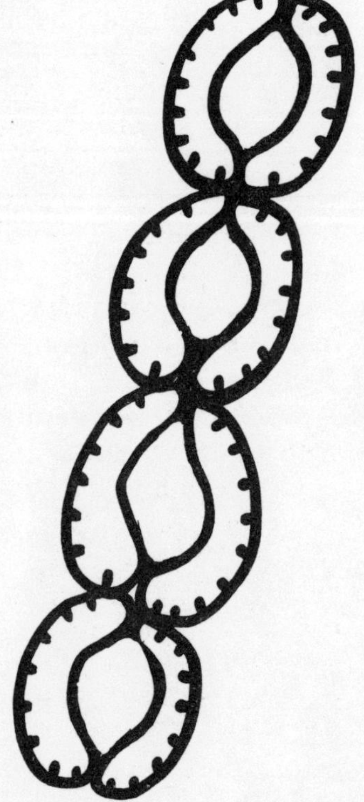

Shepherd's/Cottage Pie

This traditional dish is made with the left-overs from the Sunday roast. Shepherd's Pie uses lamb, as the name suggests. Cottage Pie uses beef. If you don't have any left-overs, you can buy minced meat.

SHEPHERD'S/ COTTAGE PIE

SERVES FOUR

450 g (1 lb) minced beef or lamb
1 onion, chopped
1 carrot, sliced
1 clove garlic, peeled and chopped
½ teaspoon dried thyme
2 teaspoons Worcestershire sauce
675 g (1½ lb) potatoes, chopped
1 tablespoon oil
2 tablespoons milk
salt
pepper
nutmeg
1 tablespoon plain flour

1. To a saucepan containing 300 ml (½ pt) of boiling water add the sliced carrot and boil for 5 mins. Keep the carrots and their water for later.
2. Heat the oil in a saucepan and, when hot, add the

onions and fry over a medium heat until just golden.

3. Add the garlic and meat and continue frying until the meat is lightly browned all over.
4. Add the carrots and their cooking water to the pan with the meat. Then add the thyme, Worcestershire sauce, salt and pepper, stir and then leave to simmer over a medium heat for 30 mins.
5. Meanwhile, put the prepared potatoes into a pot of boiling water and cook for 15 mins or until soft.
6. Drain the potatoes in a colander and return to their pot. Add the knob of butter, the milk and some grated nutmeg, then mash.
7. When the meat sauce has cooked for 30 mins transfer it to an ovenproof dish. Smooth the mashed potato over the top of the meat mixture and ripple the surface with a fork.
8. Bake in the top of a preheated oven at 180°C/300°F/gas mark 4 for 45 mins, until the top is golden brown.

Deep-Fried Fish

You'll never want to go to the fish and chip shop again!

DEEP-FRIED FISH

SERVES TWO

110 g (4 oz) plain flour
1 egg yolk
8 tablespoons semi-skimmed milk (or 4 tablespoons whole milk and 4 tablespoons water)
pinch salt
2 egg whites
2 fresh fillets fish (cod, haddock or huss), about 170–220 g (6-8 oz) each

1. Put the flour in a bowl and make a well in the centre. Add the egg yolk, salt and milk.
2. Gradually mix in the flour and stir until you have a smooth batter.
3. Leave for 30 mins.
4. In another bowl, beat the egg whites energetically with a wire whisk until they form stiff peaks. This will take a few minutes.
5. Fold the egg whites into the batter thoroughly but gently.
6. Wash the fish and pat it dry with kitchen towel.
7. Dip the fish into the batter and coat it thoroughly.
8. Place in hot oil (190°C/375°F) and deep fry (see page 75) for 5 mins, turning occasionally with a spatula, until golden brown.

Summer Pudding

We think this is one of the most delightful puddings in the world! It's simple to make and the colours are superb.

SUMMER PUDDING

SERVES SIX TO EIGHT

900 g (2 lb) fresh soft fruits (raspberries, blackberries, blackcurrants, redcurrants).
170 g (6 oz) caster sugar
Enough slices of stale white bread to line a pudding bowl

1. Pick over the fruits and remove stalks and any mouldy berries.
2. Place in a large bowl with the sugar and toss gently with a wooden spoon until the sugar has dissolved. If the fruit is not completely ripe, simmer it together with the sugar in a pan for a couple of minutes, to dissolve the sugar and bring out the juices.
3. Cover mixture and set aside.
4. Line a 1.2 litre (2 pt) pudding bowl with the bread (crusts removed), shaping a round piece for the bottom and overlapping slightly the pieces round the sides.
5. Put the fruit mixture into the lined bowl, cover it with shaped slices of bread then cover with a plate and place a heavy weight on top.
6. Leave overnight in the refrigerator.

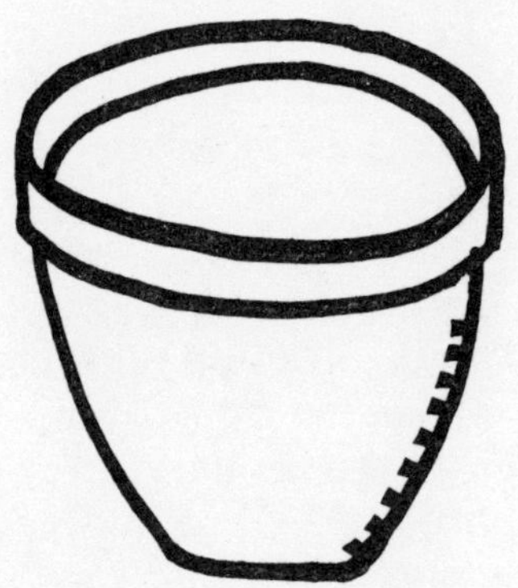

Serve with cream or Greek yoghurt.

Colin Spencer's Smoked Haddock Fishcakes

Colin Spencer is a novelist and playwright who has written a food column in the *Guardian* newspaper for the last thirteen years, as well as fifteen books on vegetarian and fish cooking. He cares passionately about the welfare of farm animals and the safeguarding of the world's resources. He is full of admiration for the many young people who are becoming vegetarian and believes that they will show more sense than their elders in caring for the planet. We hope he's right.

COLIN SPENCER'S SMOKED HADDOCK FISHCAKES

SERVES FOUR

55 g (2 oz) butter
225 g (8 oz) smoked haddock
2 large potatoes
handful of parsley, finely chopped
sea salt and freshly ground black pepper
1 egg
55 g (2 oz) toasted breadcrumbs

1. Melt the butter in a pan and place the fillet of smoked haddock skin side down in the pan with the lid on.
2. Sauté over a very low heat for 10 mins. Leave to cool, then flake the fish off the skin and give the skin to the cat (if you have one). Keep all the fish and buttery liquid.
3. Meanwhile, boil the potatoes, mash them and mix in a bowl together with the fish and liquid.
4. Add the parsley, seasoning and egg to bind the mixture. Refrigerate for 1 hr.
5. Form the mixture into small cakes and roll each one in breadcrumbs.
6. Fry these in hot oil for a few mins on both sides before serving.

Cock-a-Leekie

Scotland has many local ingredients that are the envy of the world. Fresh or smoked salmon, beef, lamb and game are all Scottish delights. The damp, cold climate makes oats rather than wheat the traditional staple. Oats are used in oatcakes and porridge and also for thickening soups, as in the recipe here.

Cock-a-Leekie is a traditional Scottish dish, first recorded in 1826. It's simple to make, full of goodness and needs to simmer for a long while.

COCK-A-LEEKIE

SERVES FOUR with left-overs

1.75 kg (4 lb) boiling fowl, skinned
1.75 kg (4 lb) leeks, well washed and chopped
12 prunes
2 tablespoons coarse oatmeal
salt to taste
1.2 litres (2 pts) beef stock (see page 115) or use stock cubes.

1. Put the skinned boiling fowl into a large pot and cover with the stock and extra water, if necessary. Bring to the boil, cover, turn the heat to low and simmer for 1½ hrs.
2. When the boiling fowl is well cooked, remove and save the stock.

3. **Add half the chopped leeks to the stock and simmer until they become a thick mass (about 1 hr).**
4. **About half an hour before you are going to eat, add the rest of the sliced leeks and 2 tablespoons of oatmeal to thicken the soup. Simmer for a final 25 mins.**
6. **Just before serving, add the prunes and the chicken cut from the carcass and salt to taste.**

Serve with fresh brown bread.

Seaweed

Different kinds of seaweed – or "sea vegetables" as they are now known – have been traditionally eaten by coastal communities all over the world. Over the last fifty years, we've sadly forgotten about these foods in Britain.

Sea vegetables are highly nutritious. They are a good source of many vitamins and minerals, provide soluble fibre and are virtually fat-free.

The many different kinds of sea vegetables have a wide variety of uses. They can enhance flavour, can add body to casseroles and stews, and can become a constituent of salads, pastas and soups. And, if soaked in water for five minutes, they can be eaten without cooking.

Sea vegetables are used extensively in Japanese cooking. The famous Japanese dish *sushi* is actually vinegared rice and raw fish wrapped in a sea vegetable called *nori*. If you get the chance, *sushi* is definitely worth trying, and it is now popular in many Western countries.

As well as being imported from countries like Japan, sea vegetables are also now farmed around the Isle of Man and off the Brittany coast. They are harvested from fresh living plants in pollution-free seas and are now available in many health-food shops in the UK.

Catherine Brown is one of Scotland's best-known food writers and has given us this traditional recipe from her book *Scottish Cookery*. It contains the sea vegetable dulse, which contains more of the mineral iron than any other food source, animal or vegetable. This broth is an excellent way of reintroducing these wonderful foods into our diet. Catherine's recipe calls for mutton, which we recommend using, but don't be put off if you can't get it as lamb also works well.

Catherine Brown's Dulse Broth with Lamb or Mutton

Catherine writes:
"This is one of the very obvious ways in which you would expect Scots to use dulse. Other meats can be used, but mutton seems more common. The dulse soup I have eaten has always been made with mutton, sometimes even the salted variety."

CATHERINE BROWN'S DULSE BROTH

SERVES FOUR

1 kg (2 lb) neck of mutton/lamb
1 onion, finely chopped
1 medium carrot, diced
3 sticks of celery, diced
2-3 medium potatoes, thinly sliced
25 g (1 oz) butter or 1 tablespoon oil
50 g (2 oz) dulse
2 litres (4 pts) water
salt and freshly ground pepper
handful of chopped parsley

1. Place the neck in a pan and add water. Bring to the boil, skim, and simmer till the meat is tender.
2. Strain cooking liquor into a bowl and remove excess surface fat – this is your stock.
3. Cut off all the edible meat from the neck and dice finely.
4. Melt the butter in a pan and add the onion. Cook till the onion is soft and yellow.
5. Add all the other vegetables and dulse and gently sweat, tightly covered, for 5-10 mins, stirring occasionally to prevent sticking.
6. Add the stock from the mutton, season, bring to the boil and simmer gently till the vegetables are cooked.
7. Just before serving, add the meat and parsley and adjust the seasoning.

22
CARIBBEAN

Caribbean cooking is constantly changing and developing. The original inhabitants of the Caribbean islands included the tribes of the Carib and Arawak peoples. Their food was a basic mixture of cassava, sweet potatoes, arrow root, guavas, cashews, pineapples and maize. The Europeans introduced breadfruit, oranges, limes, mangoes, rice, coffee and sugar cane. The many African people who were forced into the area as slaves to harvest the sugar cane, brought with them okra, callaloo (a spinach-type vegetable) and akee. After the abolition of slavery, people from China and India also came to these islands to work. All these people together influenced the region's cooking style.

One classic dish, Curry, Rice 'n' Peas, originally came from the Indian influence but the Caribbean version uses different spices, including nutmeg, cloves, cinnamon and the very Caribbean allspice. The chilli peppers used in the Caribbean, called Scotch bonnet, produce a blast of heat of nuclear proportions!

Lamb Curry

The heat of this Jamaican curry comes more from the liberal use of black pepper than the Scotch bonnet chilli pepper, which we have chosen to keep whole and remove at the end. Serve and enjoy and round it off with a fruit salad of mangoes and limes.

LAMB CURRY

SERVES FOUR TO SIX

900 g (2 lb) lamb, cut into small pieces
1½ tablespoons mild curry powder
1 teaspoon chilli powder
2 teaspoons ground allspice
2 tablespoons soy sauce
2 cloves garlic, finely chopped
2 teaspoons ground black pepper
1 bay leaf
1 sprig thyme
225 g (½ lb) onions, chopped
1 Scotch bonnet chilli pepper
225 g (½ lb) tomatoes, quartered
1 red bell pepper, de-seeded and chopped
2 tablespoons oil
300 ml (½ pt) water

1. Put the lamb in a bowl and add the curry powder, chilli powder, allspice, soy sauce, garlic, black pepper, onions and thyme.
2. Knead the lamb and powders, then leave to marinate for 1 hr.
3. Heat the oil in a saucepan over a medium heat. Add the meat mixture and cook for 10 mins.
4. Add the chopped red pepper, tomatoes, bay leaf, Scotch bonnet (whole) and water and cook for 1 hr. If the mixture starts to dry out, add more water.
5. Remove the Scotch bonnet chilli pepper before serving.

Serve with Rice 'n' Peas (see opposite).

Rice 'n' Peas

In this famous dish, the peas are in fact beans! In Jamaica red kidney beans are used, elsewhere in the Caribbean "gungo" (pigeon) peas.

RICE 'N' PEAS

SERVES FOUR TO SIX

400 g (14 oz) can red kidney beans, drained
450 g (1 lb) long grain rice
400 g (14 oz) can coconut milk or 55 g (2 oz) creamed coconut, mixed with 600 ml (1 pt) hot water
110 g (4 oz) spring onions, chopped
1 clove garlic, peeled and finely chopped
1 teaspoon black pepper
1 teaspoon salt

1. Rinse the rice several times and place in a saucepan. Add the kidney beans, can coconut milk, crushed garlic, black pepper, salt and chopped spring onions and mix well.
2. Add water to cover the rice, allowing a 2.5 cm (1 in) shelf over it, and bring to a vigorous boil. Cover with foil and a lid.
3. Turn the heat down very low and cook for 15 mins.

Serve with lamb curry and salad.

23
CHINA

The Pacific Ocean, Korea, Afghanistan and the mountainous kingdom of Nepal all lie along the borders of this vast country. Home to almost a quarter of the world's population and at well over one billion people, it's the largest country ever known.

The Chinese base their cooking on the balancing of colours, textures and what they call "the Five Flavours": salt, sweet, bitter, sour and spicy hot. This harmony, like the harmony between the two energy forces, Ying and Yang, is all-important in the appreciation of Chinese cooking. It will really challenge your taste-buds!

It's impossible to do justice here to the distinctive flavours and tastes of all the regional variations but we can make four main divisions:

The North: this region includes the capital Beijing, also called Peking, the home of the world-famous Peking Duck. The staple grain is wheat, used for noodles and bun-making, as well as rice. Garlic, spring onions, dark soy sauce and fermented black beans are among the typical seasonings of this region.

The South: with its subtropical climate and long coastline, it has a magnificent choice of seafood dishes. Cantonese food is characterised by its harmonious blending of flavours. It was the Cantonese who first brought Chinese food to the West and established Chinatowns in many Western cities. It's well known for dim sum – small snacks – and hors d'œuvres that are steamed, fried and deep fried.

The East: a land of fish and rice and the home of some of China's finest teas. It contains the city of Shanghai, once a great cosmopolitan centre, and the garden city of Suzhou, known as the Venice of China. The flavours of its food are rich and sweet due to the amount of oil, fat, sugar and wine used in the cooking.

The West: Separated by mountain ranges, this region has developed its own distinctive, highly spiced food. Fiery Szechwan peppercorns and red chillies are used extensively, giving the food its characteristic numbing and spicy hot flavours. One of the region's most famous dishes is the fantastic Hot and Sour soup and crispy fragrant duck. The Szechwan style of Chinese cooking is becoming increasingly popular in Britain.

Chinese cuisine now rivals French as the most distinguished in the world and the influence of Chinese culture and trade looks certain to grow in the next decade.

Chinese food was the first food that I learned to cook. It is a perfect introduction to cooking for young people - fun and simple to prepare, very quick to cook and full of surprises. So join us for a "wok on the wild side".

Yan-Kit So has given us two recipes from her marvellous new book *The Classic Food of China*. Her first book, *The Classic Chinese Cook Book*, was the first Chinese cookbook to win a major food award and is an excellent starting-point for anyone learning to cook the Chinese way.

Yan-Kit So's Slippery Egg with Beef Slivers

Yan-Kit writes:
"An everyday Cantonese family dish that makes for a tasty one-plate meal with rice and green vegetables. Indeed, Cantonese often serve this to their young teenage children who need as many vitamins and proteins for their growing bodies as flavours for their developing tastebuds."

YAN-KIT SO'S SLIPPERY EGG WITH BEEF SLIVERS

SERVES THREE TO FOUR
with some green vegetables

350 g (12 oz) rump or skirt steak, trimmed and cut into rectangular slivers about 6 mm (¼ in) thick
120 ml (8 tablespoons) peanut or vegetable oil
6 large eggs (size 2)
2.5 ml (½ teaspoon) salt or to taste
ground white or black pepper to taste
3-4 spring onions, green parts only, chopped into small rounds
5-10 ml (1-2 teaspoons) sesame oil

FOR THE MARINADE
2 ml (⅓ teaspoon) salt
1.5 ml (¼ teaspoon) sugar
10 ml (2 teaspoons) thin or light soy sauce
6-8 turns black pepper mill
10 ml (2 teaspoons) Shaoxing wine or medium dry sherry
7.5 ml (1½ teaspoons) cornflour
15 ml (1 tablespoon) water

1. Marinate the beef: put the slivers into a bowl and add the salt, sugar, soy sauce, pepper, wine or sherry and cornflour. Stir vigorously to coat. Add the water and stir again until totally absorbed. Leave to stand for about 20 mins.
2. Heat a wok over a high heat until smoke rises. Add the peanut or vegetable oil and swirl it around to cover a large area. Heat for about 1 min, then add the beef and stir it in the oil. Lower the heat to medium and continue to stir until the beef turns opaque, but is still underdone. Scoop on to a dish with a perforated spoon, allowing the oil to drain back into the wok. Let the beef cool off for a few minutes. (If you wish your beef to be well done, stir-fry in the oil for longer.)
3. In a large bowl beat the eggs thoroughly. Add the salt and pepper and the spring onion, mixing well. Stir in the beef.
4. Reheat the oil in the wok over a medium heat until it is hot but not smoking. Pour in the egg mixture and, with the wok scoop going to the bottom of the wok, turn and let the liquid egg go to the bottom. Repeat this action until all the liquid egg has solidified around the beef slivers. Dribble in more oil around the edges if the egg starts to stick to the wok. Transfer contents to a large serving dish and serve hot. Dribble over the sesame oil.

YAN-KIT SO'S THREE-COLOURED VEGETABLES

"The three colours are gold, white and green corresponding to carrots, bean sprouts and mangetout. This clean-looking and pretty stir-fry is designed to use the juices which exude from the bean sprouts to cook the carrots and mangetout. This last vegetable originates from Europe, and the Chinese refer to it as Holland pea, even though the rest of the world regards it as Chinese now."

SERVES FOUR with two other dishes

2 carrots, each about 50 g (2 oz)
350 g (12 oz) bean sprouts
115 g (4 oz) mangetout
45 ml (3 tablespoons) peanut or vegetable oil
4 slices ginger, peeled
3-4 spring onions, trimmed and cut diagonally at 2 cm (3/4 in) intervals, with white and green parts separated
2.5 ml (1/2 teaspoon) salt
10 ml (2 teaspoons) soy sauce

1. Peel the carrots. Make a diagonal cut at one end and then cut, either by hand or using a food processor, into slices as thin as the mangetout.
2. Bean sprouts are usually packed in pristine condition, but if you need to wash them, spin off any excess moisture.
3. Top and tail the mangetout. Wash them, rubbing off any impurities, then drain well.
4. Heat a wok over a high heat until smoke rises. Add the oil and swirl it around to cover a large area. Add the ginger, let it sizzle, then add the white spring onions and stir them several times to release the aroma. Add the bean sprouts and, going to the bottom of the wok with the wok scoop, turn and toss. Sprinkle over the salt, stir to mix, then add the carrots and mangetout and continue to stir vigorously, with the wok uncovered. The water that oozes from the bean sprouts will cook the carrots and mangetout. After stirring for 3-4 mins, the juices should be absorbed again, and the vegetables cooked yet very crunchy. Add the soy sauce, stir a few more times, add the green spring onions and stir to mix. Transfer contents to a serving dish and serve hot.

Fantastic Szechwan Chicken with Peanuts

I have been cooking this dish since I was eleven years old. It's always different and always FANTASTIC! Old friends request it when they come to stay and I can see the disappointment on their faces when I tell them we're having something else for a change.

FANTASTIC SZECHWAN CHICKEN WITH PEANUTS

SERVES FOUR with rice and salad

55 g (2 oz) peeled, fresh (unsalted) peanuts
3 chicken breasts, skinned, trimmed of fat and cut into 3 cm cubes

MARINADE
2 tablespoons light soy sauce
½ teaspoon white sugar
1 teaspoon sesame oil
1 teaspoon Chinese rice wine or dry sherry
1 egg white
1 tablespoon cornflour

SAUCE
10 cloves garlic
2 cm fresh ginger
5 dried, red chilli peppers, roughly chopped
2 large green peppers, cut into 3 x 2 cm (1½ x 1 in pieces
5 spring onions, thinly sliced crosswise
7 tablespoons peanut oil
large pinch of salt
1½ tablespoons soy sauce

If you can't get peeled, fresh peanuts you'll have to peel the red skins off yourself or ask a friend to help you.

HOW TO PEEL PEANUTS: Put peanuts into a small bowl, cover with boiling water and leave to stand for at least five minutes then drain. Squeeze the peanuts between two fingers and the skin will just pop off. This takes quite a long time but is well worth it in the final dish.

PREPARATION

1. Peel the peanuts if necessary (see box).
2. Remove all the skin, fat and bones from the chicken breasts and cut into 3-cm (1-in) cubes.
3. Put the chicken cubes into a bowl and add the marinade ingredients: soy sauce, sugar, sesame oil, rice wine or sherry, egg white and cornflour. Leave to marinate while you prepare the other ingredients.
4. Smash the garlic under the side of your cleaver or under a chopping board. Peel each clove and chop very finely. Put into a small bowl.
5. Peel the ginger and chop very finely. Add this to the bowl of garlic.
6. Roughly chop the red chilli peppers and add to the bowl with the garlic and ginger.
7. Wash the peppers, top and tail them, and remove the seeds and veins from the insides. Cut into 3 x 2 cm (1 x ¾ in) pieces and place in a bowl.
8. Wash the spring onions and finely slice both the white and green parts. Add these to the marinating chicken.

COOKING STAGE ONE - PRECOOK THE PEANUTS AND PEPPERS

1. Heat your wok or large frying pan over a medium flame for 15 secs.
2. Add 3 tablespoons of peanut oil and heat until just smoking (not burning).
3. When the oil is hot add the peanuts and stir-fry continuously until the peanuts are golden. This takes between 3 and 5 mins. The peanuts can burn easily so don't stop stirring until finished. Remove the peanuts from the pan and drain on some kitchen paper in a bowl.
4. Add the green pepper cubes to the oil left in the pan. Stir-fry over a high heat for 30 secs.
5. Add a large pinch of salt and stir-fry for an extra minute.
6. Remove the peppers from the pan and drain on kitchen paper.
7. Remove the pan from the heat. When cool enough to handle, wipe the surface of the pan with kitchen paper until clean.

COOKING STAGE TWO - THE FINAL STAGE

This final stage only takes 5 mins so make sure everything else is ready: the rice is cooked, the table set, the salad made and all the ingredients for the final dish lined up next to the stove. Once you start stir-frying you won't have time to dash around the kitchen looking for things. Always be well prepared before you begin.

Check list - here is a list of your ingredients in their order of use:

* bowl of garlic, ginger and chilli
* bowl of chicken, spring onions and marinade
* bowl of precooked green peppers
* 1½ tablespoons of soy sauce, measured out in a bowl
* bowl of cooked peanuts

Get everything ready and wok on...

1. Heat the wok over a high flame for 15 secs.
2. Add 4 tablespoons of peanut oil.
3. Test that the oil is the right temperature by adding a little piece of ginger to it. If the ginger sinks, it's too cold, if it burns, it's too hot, if it floats on the surface bubbling and hissing, it's just right.
4. When the oil is hot add the garlic, ginger and chilli mix, and stir-fry very quickly for 30 secs. Don't let it burn.
5. Quickly add the chicken mixture and stir-fry for another minute and a half or until the chicken pieces begin to firm up.
6. Add the green peppers and stir-fry for another minute.
7. Add the soy sauce and cooked peanuts and stir-fry for 15 secs.

HOT AND SOUR CUCUMBER SALAD

SERVES FOUR

1 large cucumber
2 teaspoons salt
1½ tablespoons white wine vinegar
3 tablespoons sugar
1 tablespoon sesame oil
½ tablespoon peanut oil
2 dried red chillies, de-seeded and chopped

1. Quarter the cucumber lengthways, scoop out and discard the seeds, then cut into bite-sized chunks.
2. Put the chunks into a bowl, sprinkle with salt, stir and leave for 2 hrs.
3. Drain the cucumber and get rid of any excess moisture.
4. Put the cucumber in a clean bowl, add the vinegar and sugar and mix well.
5. Heat the oils in a small saucepan until smoke rises. Remove the pan from the heat and after a few seconds add the chillies and let them sizzle. Pour them into the bowl with the cucumber and mix well.
6. Leave to stand for at least 6 hrs to mingle flavours.

---

24 FRANCE

France is famous all over the world for its good food. We've even adopted into our language several French terms for food and cooking such as sauté, pâté, hors d'oeuvre and, of course, cuisine. When the Italian princess, Catherine de Medici came to France in 1533 to marry the French king-to-be, she brought her Italian chefs with her. They were regarded as the greatest chefs of their time, and consequently French cuisine advanced by leaps and bounds. In 1651, Careme published the first book to record the rules and principles of cooking.

Heavily spiced foods became less popular and the great French chefs became increasingly imaginative. They discovered how to make stocks to flavour their soups and sauces. By the twentieth century France was universally acclaimed as having the best cuisine in the world. (Not everyone would agree with that today!)

Escoffier, one of the great chefs of the twentieth century, said that the whole of French cooking stood or fell by its use of essential stock and the five basic sauces: béchamel, velouté, tomato, hollandaise and espagnole (see page 115). His most important piece of advice was: "Make it simple."

Ratatouille

A Provençale vegetable dish made during the summer months when these vegetables are at their best and cheapest.

RATATOUILLE

SERVES FOUR

225 g (½ lb) onions, chopped
225 g (½ lb) green peppers, de-seeded and chopped
225 g (½ lb) aubergines, sliced 2 cm (¾ in) thick
225 g (½ lb) courgettes, sliced 2 cm (½ in) thick
400 g (14 oz) can plum tomatoes
2 cloves garlic, peeled and chopped
a few leaves fresh basil
8 tablespoons olive oil
1 teaspoon salt
1 teaspoon black pepper

1. Put 2 tablespoons of the olive oil in a frying pan over a medium heat and add the aubergines. Lightly brown them on both sides and then place in a saucepan over a low heat.
2. Repeat this process with the onions and garlic, and place on top of the aubergines.
3. Repeat process again with the peppers, and place on top of the onions.
4. Repeat finally with the courgettes, and place on top of the peppers. Add the salt, pepper and basil to the saucepan
5. To the frying pan add the tomatoes and cook for 5 mins to lose some of the watery liquid, then add to the saucepan.
6. Gently mix together ingredients, then cover and continue cooking for 20 mins.

This dish can be served either hot or cold.

TROUT SAUTÉED IN BUTTER

SERVES TWO

2 trout (about 225 g or 8 oz each), gutted
30 g (1 oz) butter
1 tablespoon olive oil
flour
salt
lemon slices

1. Wash the trout in cold water and dry them thoroughly with paper towel.
2. Sprinkle a little salt inside and outside the trout, dip them in some flour and shake off the excess.
3. Melt the butter and oil in a heavy frying pan over a moderate heat. When the foam starts to subside add the trout and sauté over a high heat for 5 mins on each side.

Serve immediately garnished with lemon slices.

STOCK

Basic Meat Stock

2 chicken carcasses (chopped) or 450 g (1 lb) soup beef and 900 g (2 lb) beef bones
1 onion, halved
1 carrot
1 celery stalk (including leaf), chopped
bouquet garni

1. Put the chicken or beef in a saucepan and cover with 2.5 cm (1 in) of water. Bring to the boil and skim off the scum that appears.
2. Add the vegetables and bouquet garni, turn the heat to low, cover saucepan and cook for 2-3 hrs.
3. Remove the bones and strain the stock through a sieve into a bowl.
4. Refrigerate until the fat solidifies and can be removed.

This stock will keep for 3 days in the refrigerator or can be frozen.

Basic Vegetable Stock

Vegetable stock can be the water saved after cooking vegetables or it can be made from fresh vegetables and the scraps – tips, tops, trimmings, peelings, roots – and fresh herb stems.

ROUX

45 g (1½ oz) butter
45 g (1½ oz) flour

1. Melt the butter in a heavy saucepan.
2. Add the flour, stir briskly until you have a smooth mixture, and continue to cook for 1 min.

White Sauce

3. Gradually add 450 ml (¾ pt) hot milk, stirring briskly the whole time to stop any lumps forming.
4. When the liquid comes to the boil remove from heat.

(Now you can choose what flavour, if any, you wish.)

Cheese Sauce

5. Add 55 g (2 oz) grated cheese (Cheddar, Parmesan or Gruyère), a pinch of nutmeg, salt and pepper and stir for a minute or so until the cheese melts.

If the sauce is lumpy force it through a fine sieve and simmer for 5 mins.

To make Béchamel Sauce, follow the recipe for White Sauce using milk flavoured with onion, parsley, peppercorns and bay leaf.

Other sauces can be made by substituting stock for milk and then adding parsley or mustard.

Vichy Carrots

Vichy carrots were so called because they used to be cooked in Vichy mineral water.

VICHY CARROTS

SERVES FOUR as a side-dish

450 g (1 lb) new carrots, sliced
30 g (1 oz) butter
1 teaspoon sugar
1 teaspoon salt
water

1. Melt the butter in a saucepan and add the carrots, sugar and salt. Add just enough water to cover and cook over a low heat until all the liquid has been absorbed or has evaporated.

Garlic Bread

One theory about the origin of garlic bread is that wild garlic grew amongst the wheat and was not always weeded out before harvesting, thus giving the milled wheat a garlic flavour.

GARLIC BREAD

1 stick of French bread
110 g (4 oz) butter
6 large cloves garlic, peeled and minced

Preheat oven to 180°C/350°F/gas mark 4.

1. Blend the butter and garlic together until smooth.
2. Slice the stick at 5 cm (2 in) intervals nearly all the way through and put a little garlic mixture in each cut.
3. Wrap the stick in foil and place in the oven for 10 mins.

25 INDIA

India is a huge and fascinating country of many different races and regions - from the lush, green meadows of Kashmir and the deserts of Rajasthan to the tropical paradises of the South. This great variety is reflected in the cooking styles of these different regions.

Spices play a vital role in Indian food. Some are grown there, like pepper, cardamom and ginger, which comes from the South. Others are imported: cloves, nutmeg and mace from Indonesia and coriander and cumin from the Middle East. Indian food is often very hot but amazingly it wasn't until the sixteenth century that hot chillies arrived from the New World of America. But don't be put off if you don't like hot food. You can make very good mild curries too.

Large parts of India, especially southern India, are vegetarian due to the religious influences of Buddhism and Jainisim. The Muslims don't eat pork and the Hindus don't eat either pork or beef.

The regions of the North West, such as Kashmir, were influenced by the Greeks and the Aryans from Persia (Iran) who introduced ghee (clarified butter) and dairy products to India. The North West is a very fertile region with rich pastures perfect for the grazing of dairy herds. The Persians were also responsible for making the cow sacred, and forbidding the consumption of beef. This dietary law was introduced to protect the dairy cow because she was more valuable for her milk than her meat.

Dairy products still play an important role in the diet of India. Yoghurt and cheese are widely used in many dishes such as the refreshing yoghurt raitas which accompany many meals.

Coconut Chicken Curry

Curries don't come any easier to make than this. This one is delicious served with rice, sweet chutney and raita.

COCONUT CHICKEN CURRY

SERVES FOUR

1.35 kg (3 lb) chicken, skinned and cut into portions (ask your butcher to prepare the chicken for you, and retain the carcass for the stock)
4 tablespoons sunflower oil
3 medium onions, chopped
2 cloves garlic, peeled and chopped
2 tablespoons Madras curry powder
2 tablespoons white wine vinegar
600 ml (1 pt) chicken stock (made from the chicken carcass)
55 g (2 oz) creamed coconut (this comes in a hard bar, a bit like soap), chopped

MAKE STOCK

1. Put the chicken carcass in a saucepan, add 1.2 litres (2 pts) water, bring to the boil over a high heat, turn the heat to low, cover and simmer for 1 hr. Remove from the heat and strain through a sieve to remove the bones. This liquid is your chicken stock.
2. Put 2 tablespoons of the oil in a large frying pan over a medium heat, add the onions and garlic and sauté for about 15 mins or until the onions turn a golden colour.
3. Mix the curry powder with the vinegar to make a curry paste.
4. Add the curry paste to the frying pan and stir for 2 mins, until the odours are released.
5. Add the chicken pieces and brown slightly for 10 mins, occasionally turning the pieces over and scraping the pan with a spatula to stop the spices sticking to the pan.
6. While the chicken is cooking make up the coconut milk by dissolving the creamed coconut in a little hot stock (150 ml or ¼ pt).
7. Add the coconut liquid and about another 450 ml (¾ pt) of the stock to the pan with the chicken. (If your frying pan isn't large enough, transfer everything to a saucepan once the chicken has browned. Rinse out the frying pan with the coconut liquid before adding it to the chicken, to ensure none of the flavour is lost.)

8. Turn the heat to low and simmer for 1 hr. If the chicken starts to become dry add a little more stock.

Serve with rice, salad and the banana raita on page 121.

Note:
It's fine to cook curries the day before they are needed and to reheat them the following day when the flavours will have matured.

SPICES

The main spices used in Indian curry powder are:

Coriander seeds
Cumin seeds
Fennel seeds
Black pepper
Cardamom pods
Cloves
Cinnamon sticks
Turmeric
Fenugreek
Ground ginger

Chilli - This is a major ingredient in curry powder but we prefer to keep it separate from the spice mix, so that you can alter the heat of the dish from day to day.

Coriander is the main ingredient (up to fifty per cent of the total mix) followed by cumin, fennel, black pepper or turmeric. The more aromatic fenugreek, cloves, cinnamon and cardamom are used in much smaller quantities.

SPICE MIXES - GRIND IT

The curry powder you used in the Coconut Chicken Curry is actually a mixture of many different spices. Although these shop-bought mixes are convenient, making your own spice mixtures at home is much more exciting. As you learn to mix the different spices yourself, you will be able to make a dish taste exactly how you like it. So get mixing!

When you start to make your own spice mixes try to buy the spices whole, not ground. It's much better to grind them just before cooking, because they begin to lose their flavour after they have been ground. Whole spices need to be roasted before they are ground and the easiest way to do this is in a dry frying pan. Heat them over a medium heat for about three minutes or until the smell or aroma of the spices is released. Stir occasionally to make sure they don't burn. Once the aroma is released, remove from the heat. The spices are now ready to grind either in an old coffee grinder or by hand, with a pestle and mortar.

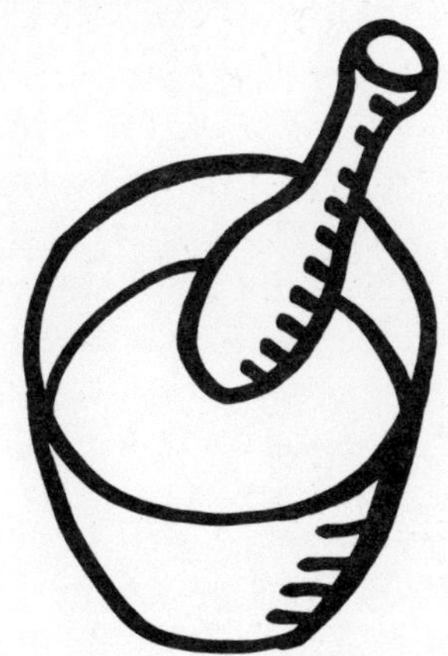

Sag Aloo (Spinach and Potatoes)

This classic dish is cooked in many different ways all over India.

SAG ALOO

SERVES FOUR as a side-dish.

2 tablespoons oil
1 medium onion, chopped
1 clove garlic, peeled and chopped
½ teaspoon fresh ginger root, chopped
½ teaspoon turmeric
½ teaspoon salt
½ teaspoon paprika
½ teaspoon ground coriander
225 g (½ lb) potatoes, peeled and chopped into bite-sized pieces
225 g (½ lb) spinach leaves, fresh or defrosted from frozen

1. Heat the oil in a frying pan over a medium heat. Add the onion, garlic and ginger and sauté for 5 mins.
2. Add the other spices and sauté for another 2 mins.
3. Add the chopped potatoes and fry for 10 mins or until slightly crispy, stirring occasionally.
4. Add the spinach leaves and continue to cook and stir until the potatoes are cooked all the way through. Make sure the potatoes do not overcook and start falling apart.

Bhindi (Okra or Lady's Fingers)

This is a small side-dish that contains the spice mix known as garam masala.

GARAM MASALA is a mixture of spices that is normally made up of ground cardamom, cinnamon, black peppercorns, coriander, cumin, cloves and nutmeg. It is often added at the end of the cooking time in much the same way as we use salt and pepper.

BHINDI

SERVES FOUR as a small side-dish

225 g (½ lb) okra
2 tablespoons oil
1 onion, chopped
2 cloves garlic, peeled and chopped
½ teaspoon salt
¼ teaspoon turmeric
½ teaspoon garam masala
½ teaspoon paprika
150 ml (¼ pt) yoghurt
100 ml (4 fl oz) water
fresh coriander leaves

1. Wash the okra and cut off the stalks.
2. Heat all the oil in a frying pan over a medium heat. When hot, add the okra and fry until golden.

3. Remove the okra from the pan and set aside.
4. In the same oil and pan, sauté the onion and garlic until golden.
5. Add the spices and cook for a few more minutes.
6. Add the yoghurt and stir, then add the water.
7. Simmer gently for 10 mins.

The sauce can now be turned off until you are ready to serve.

8. 5 mins before serving, reheat the yoghurt sauce until simmering.
9. Add the prepared okra and simmer until the okra is warmed through, about 2 mins.
10. Put in a serving bowl and garnish with a few freshly chopped coriander leaves.

NB Don't chop the coriander until just before serving as it quickly loses its high vitamin C content.

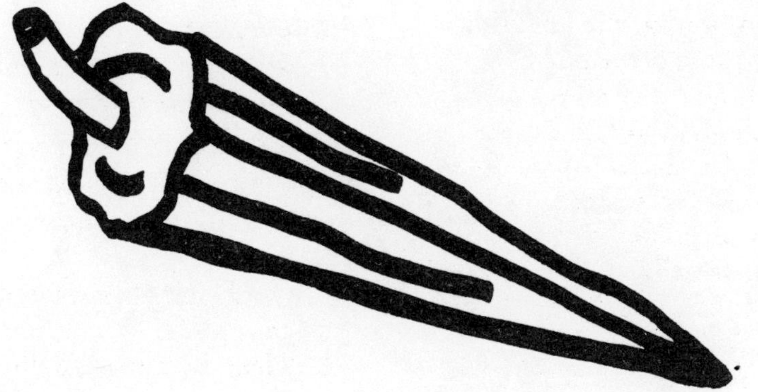

ONION RAITA

100 ml (4 fl oz) plain yoghurt
1 medium onion , grated
paprika
a few chopped mint leaves

1. Mix the onion and yoghurt in a bowl and then garnish with the mint leaves and a pinch of paprika.

BANANA RAITA

1 banana, sliced
juice of 1 lemon
100 ml (4 fl oz) plain yoghurt
pinch of paprika

1. Pour the lemon juice over the bananas in a bowl.
2. Add the yoghurt and mix together.
3. Garnish with a pinch of paprika.

26
ITALY

Italian food is very popular in Britain and has a long and distinguished history. It's known as the Mother of European cuisine. Records show that the Romans invented cheesecake! In the ninth century, the Arabs arrived and introduced the art of ice-cream making for which the Italians are still celebrated. The famous explorer, Marco Polo, who travelled to China, opened up the spice route to the East and Venice became the main spice centre of Europe. It's said that he discovered spaghetti in China but this is a myth.

Tomatoes, which are a key ingredient in Italian cooking, were brought back by explorers from Peru to Italy in the sixteenth century. Called the "pomo d'oro" or "golden apple", the tomato was originally thought to be poisonous. It wasn't until two centuries later that the Italians discovered its properties as a versatile vegetable/fruit. They were also the first in Europe to exploit maize as a food.

These days the Mediterranean diet of southern Italy is considered to be extremely healthy with its generous use of olive oil, its high carbohydrate content and wealth of fruit and vegetables. It's also the home of a great variety of quick, cheap and terrific meals such as pizza and pasta. And you can round them off with cheesecake or ice-cream!

ROMAN CHEESECAKE

SERVES EIGHT

PASTRY

110 g (4 oz) plain flour
85 g (3 oz) unsalted butter
2 egg yolks
1 tablespoon caster sugar
grated lemon rind
1 tablespoon water
pinch of salt

FILLINGS

450 g (1 lb) ricotta cheese
2 tablespoons caster sugar
2 teaspoons plain flour
1 teaspoon vanilla essence
grated rind 1 orange
grated rind 1 lemon
juice of 1 lemon
2 egg yolks
1 tablespoon sultanas
pinch of salt
2 egg whites

1. Put the flour, butter and sugar in a bowl and mix with your fingertips until they form a crumbly mixture.
2. Add the egg yolks,water, lemon rind and salt and beat thoroughly with a wooden spoon until the mixture sticks together in a lump.
3. Refrigerate for 1 hr.
4. Flour a board, flatten the ball of pastry on it and roll out until it will fit an 18 cm (7 in) baking tin with a depth of 5 cm (2 in).
5. Gently lift the pastry and place it over the tin, pressing down gently around the sides. Trim off any excess with a knife.
6. Preheat an oven to 180°C/350°F/gas mark 4.
7. Put all the filling ingredients except the egg whites into a bowl and beat with a wooden spoon until thoroughly mixed.
8. In a separate bowl whisk the egg whites until they form stiff peaks, then gently fold into the ricotta mixture.
9. Spoon the mixture into the pastry shell and level it off with a spatula.
10. Bake in the middle of the oven for 50 mins.

An easier alternative to the pastry shell is crumbled digestive biscuits. Grease the baking tin liberally with butter. Break the biscuits up, place in a paper bag and crush with a rolling pin. Spread the crumbs over the base of the tin, turn the tin on its side and roll around until the sides are covered then proceed as above.

Spaghetti Carbonara (Egg and Bacon Spaghetti)

The egg and bacon of breakfast fame are combined here with freshly grated Parmesan and spaghetti to make this famous dish from Rome, the capital of Italy. It is tasty, quick to make and very filling – perfect for when you're tired and hungry.

Because this dish is as easy to make for one as it is for a crowd we have included quantities for four people as well as for one. As you can see the ingredients don't just double to increase quantities. Although you need one egg for one person and two for two, you need only three eggs for four people and four eggs for six.

SPAGHETTI CARBONARA

SERVES FOUR

55 g (2 oz) freshly grated Parmesan cheese
3 eggs
170-225 g (6-8oz) smoked bacon or smoked ham for a milder taste, or a mixture of both
1 tablespoon olive oil
lots of freshly ground pepper

2 tablespoons freshly chopped parsley
110-140 g (4-5 oz) spaghetti per person
at least 3 litres (5 pts) water

PER PERSON
1 tablespoon freshly grated Parmesan cheese
1 egg
2-3 rashers smoked bacon or smoked ham, or a bit of both
1 teaspoon olive oil
lots of freshly ground pepper
1 teaspoon freshly chopped parsley
110-140 g (4-5 oz) spaghetti, how hungry are you!
at least 3 litres (5 pts) of water

1. Bring the water to the boil in a large saucepan.
2. Remove the rind from the bacon and chop finely, or cut rashers into strips.
3. Heat the olive oil in a frying pan and when hot add the bacon pieces, sauté, stirring occasionally, and turn off when crispy.
4. While the bacon is cooking check that the water is boiling vigorously. Add the spaghetti and stir until all the strands are separate. Cover the pan to bring quickly back to the boil, uncover and cook until just al dente, stirring occasionally.
5. While the spaghetti is cooking break the egg(s) into a bowl and whisk until fluffy. Add the grated Parmesan cheese and mix with a fork until well combined. Add the freshly ground pepper to the egg mixture.
6. When the spaghetti is just al dente, drain in a colander and return to its pan over a very low heat.
7. QUICKLY add the egg mixture, crispy bacon bits from the frying pan and chopped parsley.
8. Mix the contents of the pan together over a low heat until the egg thickens. Don't overcook or the egg will scramble and separate.
9. Serve immediately straight from the pan or from a preheated serving bowl.

Serve with Basic Green Salad.

VARIATION
Instead of bacon substitute fried courgettes, a red and a green pepper and mozzarella cheese.

1. Wash and slice the courgettes and peppers.
2. Sauté them in olive oil over a medium heat until slightly golden.
3. Cut the mozzarella into small cubes and set aside.
4. Follow the above recipe until stage 7.
5. QUICKLY add the chopped

mozzarella, courgettes and peppers from the frying pan, egg mixture and chopped parsley.
6. Mix the contents together until the mozzarella begins to melt and the egg thickens. Do not overcook or the egg will scramble and separate.

Serve as above.

DIY Fresh Fettuccine

Making your own pasta is simple and very satisfying. The texture and price of this pasta is a great improvement on the expensive shop-bought fresh pastas. It's good with a simple olive oil, fresh basil and garlic dressing.

This recipe is for two people. To make more, don't just increase the quantities, make more batches of the same size – two batches for four people and so on. We don't recommend making more than two batches at one go unless you've got strong arms or lots of friends to help with the rolling.

DIY FRESH FETTUCCINE

TO MAKE PASTA
6 oz plain flour
2 eggs
2 teaspoons olive oil
1 teaspoon salt
1 teaspoon water

TO MAKE DRESSING
4 tablespoons olive oil
2 cloves garlic, peeled and very finely chopped
½ oz fresh basil, chopped
1 oz Parmesan cheese, grated
freshly ground black pepper

MAKING THE FETTUCCINE
1. Put the flour into a large mixing bowl and scoop a well or hole in the centre big enough to hold the other ingredients.
2. Crack the eggs into the well, add the oil and salt and mix together until the dough forms a loose ball. (Add a few drops of water to help pick up any loose bits of dough still in the bowl.)
3. Move your ball of dough to a clean, floured surface where you can start kneading. (See kneading on page 54.)
4. Knead the dough for about 10 mins, until it is smooth and elastic. You may need to add a little more flour if the dough is sticky, or a few drops of water if it is too dry and hard. All flours are different so use your judgement. After kneading leave the dough to rest for 15 mins.
5. When the dough is ready divide it into two balls of equal size.
6. Using a rolling pin, roll the dough ball into the shape of a large rectangle – it should be almost paper-thin. Dust the dough and rolling

surface with flour to stop them sticking. While rolling the dough out, occasionally roll it around the rolling pin, lift it from the surface, turn it half way round and roll again, then repeat. If the dough begins to stick, dust it with more flour.

7. When you have rolled out the dough, dust the top surface and roll the dough into itself like a Swiss roll or rolled-up poster. You must do this gently to prevent the dough from sticking to itself.
8. Slice your roll of pasta into thin rounds. You can choose the thickness – fettuccine is normally about ¾ cm wide.
9. As soon as all the rounds are cut, lift them in the air by one end. They should fall out into a long strand like a party streamer. Lay each finished fettuccine out on a clean surface so that they do not touch each other.
10. Repeat steps 6, 7, 8 and 9 with the second ball of dough.

TO MAKE SAUCE

1. Put the finely chopped garlic and olive oil into a small saucepan and heat up over a medium heat.
2. As soon as the garlic begins to sizzle turn off the heat and add the chopped basil. Leave the sauce to infuse while you cook the pasta.

COOKING THE FETTUCCINE

1. Bring at least 3.5 litres (6 pints) of water to boil in a large saucepan.
2. When the water is boiling vigorously add the fettuccine and stir gently to prevent the strands from sticking.
3. The pasta will be cooked in about 5-8 mins, depending on how thick the strands are. It should be al dente – firm to the bite but not floury or chalky. Avoid overcooking.
4. Drain the pasta immediately in a colander and return to the hot pan or a preheated serving dish.
5. Immediately add the prepared olive oil, garlic and basil mixture together with the Parmesan cheese. Toss well, season with lots of black pepper and eat at once.

Serve with a crispy, green salad.

27 JEWISH FOOD

Jewish cuisine is a truly international cuisine and we wanted to include a sample of its food. We asked Evelyn Rose, author of *The New Complete International Jewish Cook Book,* to suggest some recipes. She gave us these three excellent recipes together with this introduction to Jewish food and the principles on which it is based.

Evelyn writes:
"Jewish cuisine is one of the most varied in the world. Throughout the centuries as the Jewish people were forced to move from country to country to avoid persecution, they adopted and adapted many of the recipes and ingredients they found in their new homelands such as Spain, Germany, Poland, Russia and the Middle East.

"However, they chose only those dishes that conformed with the strict Jewish dietary laws that tradition has it were given to the Jewish women by Moses on Mount Sinai.

"In addition, many dishes were chosen because they could be cooked on Friday and can either be kept hot overnight or served cold on the Sabbath when cooking is not allowed: or they are suitable to be served at a special meal at one of the many festivals that are celebrated each year.

"In general, Jewish food is simple to prepare, tasty and economical - like the three wonderful dishes I give below."

Evelyn Rose's Honey Lekach

"This light and spongy cake with its wonderfully moist texture is eaten in every Jewish home at the time of the new year - Rosh Hashanah. At this festival, it is customary to eat sweet foods, containing honey and dried fruits in particular, as a symbol of hope for a sweet - and happy - year ahead."

EVELYN ROSE'S HONEY LEKACH

175 g (6 oz) plain flour
75 g (3 oz) caster sugar
½ teaspoon ground ginger
½ teaspoon ground cinnamon
1 level teaspoon mixed spice
225 g (8 oz) clear honey
4 tablespoons sunflower oil
2 eggs
1 level teaspoon bicarbonate of soda dissolved in 75 ml (3 fl oz) orange juice
grated rind of the orange
50 g (2 oz) chopped walnuts
Preheat oven to 180°C / 350°F / gas mark 4.

1. Mix together the flour, sugar and spices.
2. Make a well in the centre, then add the honey, oil, rind and eggs. Beat together until smooth.
3. Dissolve the bicarbonate of soda in the orange juice and add the nuts. Stir this into the flour mixture.
4. Pour into a greaseproof- or silicon-paper-lined tin of approx 25 x 20 x 5 cm (10 x 8 x 2 in).
5. Bake in the preheated oven for 50-55 mins, or until firm to the touch.
6. Remove from the oven and leave to cool. When quite cold, remove from the tin, wrap in tin foil and leave at room temperature for 4-5 days, if possible, before using. It improves with keeping.

NB This cake keeps for two weeks at room temperature in an airtight container or for three months in the freezer.

Evelyn Rose's Spinach and Cheese Eggah

"This baked omelette is a favourite dish of those Jews who once lived in Middle Eastern countries such as Egypt, Syria and the Lebanon. It is very similar to the Spanish tortilla, though who thought of it first - the Moors who once lived in Spain, or the Spaniards - nobody knows. It can be served either warm - it makes a delicious vegetarian main course - or cold, when it's super for a picnic."

EVELYN ROSE'S SPINACH AND CHEESE EGGAH

SERVES FOUR TO FIVE as a main meal or EIGHT TO TEN as a snack

3 eggs
4 tablespoons creamy milk
1 small packet frozen leaf spinach (approx 125 g or 4 oz when defrosted and well drained)
1 small onion, chopped
25 g (1 oz) butter
125 g (4 oz) mushrooms, sliced
175 g (6 oz) grated Cheddar cheese
1 level tablespoon chopped parsley or scissored chives
salt
black pepper

1. Sauté the onion in the butter until soft and golden.
2. Add the sliced mushrooms and cook until the butter is absorbed (about 2 or 3 mins).
3. Beat the eggs until blended, then add the milk, herbs, seasonings, spinach, onion, mushrooms and cheese.
4. Butter a 23 cm (9 in) diameter ovenproof casserole with a depth of about 5 cm (2 in), or use a tin or foil container of similar depth, measuring about 25 x 18 cm (10 x 7 in).
5. Pour in the mixture and bake in a preheated oven at 190°C / 375° F / gas mark 5 for 30 mins, until set and golden.
6. Serve cut into sections when warm, or cut into small squares and spear on cocktail sticks to serve cold.

Evelyn Rose's Izmir Keufteh (Smyrna Meatballs)

"Many Jewish families fled to Turkey when they were expelled from Spain in 1492. Although they still continued to cook Spanish dishes, they soon adopted some from the cuisine of the Turkish Ottoman Empire, such as this delicious dish of tender meatballs simmered in a mouthwatering sweet and sour tomato sauce".

EVELYN ROSE'S IZMIR KEUFTEH

SERVES SIX TO EIGHT
Halve the quantities for three to four but cook for the same length of time.

FOR MEAT MIXTURE
2 slices of bread, each cut 2.5 cm (1 in) thick
2 large eggs
half a large onion
1 large sprig parsley (optional)
1 level teaspoon salt
15 grinds black pepper
3 teaspoons dark soy sauce
900 g (2 lb) raw minced beef

FOR THE SAUCE
1 medium onion
2 tablespoons oil
30 g (1 oz) pine kernels (optional but nice)
150 g (5 oz) can tomato purée and 2 cans water
juice of half a large lemon
1 level tablespoon brown sugar
salt
pepper

To prepare the minced beef mixture:

By hand: soak the bread in water to cover, then squeeze dry and add to the beaten eggs, grated onion, herbs (if used) and seasonings.

By blender or food processor: put the fresh herbs, unbeaten eggs, slices of bread, chunks of onion and seasonings into the blender or food processor and process for 30 secs or until smooth.

In both cases work together the raw meat and the egg mixture with the hand or a large fork, until smoothly blended. Leave for 30 mins. The mixture can now be formed into patties or balls.

While the minced meat is standing, cut the onion in half and then cut into very thin slices. Heat the oil in a deepish frying pan or casserole, add the onion and cook gently for about 5 mins, until limp.

Meanwhile, shape the meat into "golf balls", add to the pan (in two lots if necessary) and cook gently until golden brown. If pine kernels are used, add them and cook for 2 mins until golden.

Now add the remaining sauce ingredients and bring to the boil (the meatballs should be barely covered - if not, add a little more water). Cover and simmer for 1 hr.

Garnish with freshly chopped parsley.

28 MEXICO

The cooking of Mexico is a wonderful mix of old and new. The now-famous tacos, tortilla, enchiladas and refried beans all have their roots in an exciting period of history.

When European explorers arrived in Mexico they found it was inhabited by the people of the Aztec and Mayan civilisations. These amazing people had already learnt how to cultivate crops and understood the importance of conservation and the principles of a balanced diet (something many of us still fail to grasp today).

The Aztecs and Mayans grew corn, beans and marrows in the same fields. The beans grew up the stalks of the corn and the marrows grew in between. This gave them all the nutrients they needed and at the same time maintained the fertility of the land. They also bred turkeys and kept bees for honey. They were careful not to over-hunt the deer and other wild animals, conserving them by regulating their hunts.

All their food was either boiled, steamed or roasted. They did not use fat for cooking. It was the Spanish who brought over pigs, lard and frying. If you look at any Mexican cookbook you will see that whenever a recipe calls for fat it is nearly always lard (pig fat).

You may have noticed by now that we are chilli pepper fans, and we are very envious of the wide varieties of chillies that grow in Mexico. People tend to think of chillies as just being HOT. But the Mexicans grow many kinds with a wide range of heat and flavours. Some are very hot, others almost sweet. They often incorporate three of four different types in one dish.

Sadly, many of these mouthwatering varieties of chilli are not available in this country. Try experimenting with all the different ones you can find. Fresh, dried, canned or even pickled chillies make a welcome change from the blow-your-head-off chilli powders generally available.

BLACK BEAN SOUP

SERVES FOUR

225 g (8 oz) dried black beans
1.25 litres (2 pts) water
1 bay leaf
2 tablespoons oil or lard
1 onion, finely chopped
1 clove garlic, peeled and finely chopped
2 tomatoes, peeled and chopped
½ teaspoon salt
½ teaspoon dried oregano
1 small dried red chilli

Garnish: chopped fresh chilli pepper and chopped spring onion

1. Soak the beans in plenty of water overnight.
2. Drain the beans then place in a large saucepan with the measured water and bay leaf. Heat over a high heat until boiling, then reduce the heat to low and simmer, covered, for 1½ hrs.
3. Meanwhile, heat the oil in a frying pan, add the onion and garlic and sauté for 4 mins.
4. Add the tomato, salt, oregano and chilli and cook over a medium heat until the mixture is almost dry.
5. Add the tomato mixture to the beans, stir and simmer, covered, for another 30 mins.
6. Mash the beans roughly and serve.

Garnish with chopped fresh green chillies and chopped spring onions.
Cut limes into wedges and squeeze juice over the soup.

REFRIED BEANS

SERVES FOUR

225 g (8 oz) dried beans (pinto or kidney)
3 tablespoons oil or lard
1 onion, sliced
1 onion, finely chopped
1 clove garlic, peeled and finely chopped
1 litre (1¾ pts) water

Garnish: grated Cheddar cheese

1. Soak the beans in plenty of water overnight.
2. Drain the beans and put them into a saucepan with 1 tablespoon of the oil, the sliced onion, and 1 litre (1¾ pts) water. Bring to the boil over a high heat and boil rapidly for 15 mins. Then reduce the heat to low and simmer, covered, for 2 hrs.
3. Heat the oil in a frying pan, add the onion and garlic and sauté over a medium heat for 4 mins.

4. Turn the heat to high, add some of the cooked beans and mash and cook until they begin to dry. Add some more beans and repeat until all have been added and the mixture is a purée.
5. Put the beans on a serving dish and garnish with grated cheese.

Serve with cos lettuce leaves, radishes, tortilla chips, salsa and guacamole.

SALSA

450 g (1 lb) tomatoes
1 onion, finely chopped
1 tablespoon fresh coriander leaves, finely chopped
1 small green chilli, seeded and chopped (optional)
pinch of salt
pinch of sugar
pinch of pepper

1. Put the tomatoes in a bowl and pour boiling water over them. This is the key to peeling tomatoes easily. After 15 secs drain them, run some cold water over them and, with a knife, make a nick to break the skin and start peeling.
2. Cut the tomatoes in half, remove the seeds and chop the flesh finely.
3. Put the tomato flesh and the rest of the ingredients in a bowl and mix together gently.

GUACAMOLE

3 ripe avocados
½ onion, finely chopped
1 small, fresh green chilli, seeded and finely chopped
1 tomato, peeled, seeded and coarsely chopped
1 tablespoon fresh coriander leaves, finely chopped
pinch of salt
pinch of pepper

1. Halve the avocados and remove the stones.
2. Scoop out the flesh, put in a bowl and mash with a fork.
3. Add all the other ingredients and mix together gently.
4. Cover with cling film and refrigerate for 1-2 hrs.

29
THE MIDDLE EAST

Claudia Roden wrote her first book on Middle Eastern cooking, *A Book of Middle Eastern Food*, twenty-five years ago, the year I was born. It is still a classic. As well as giving us three recipes, she explains the essence of Middle Eastern cookery:

"Although every country and every town in the Middle East has its own special dishes, there are many similarities in the cooking. You find kebabs - meats threaded on skewers and grilled over charcoal – everywhere. You also find pilafs – rice cooked with other ingredients such as bits of chicken or lamb with pine nuts and raisins; every kind of stuffed vegetable; little packets of folded pastry with cheese inside; thick cake-like omelettes filled with vegetables; milk puddings and pastries stuffed with nuts and soaked in syrup. This is because the countries have all been part of empires which spread across the whole region and they have had the same influences.

"Middle Eastern cooking is based on vegetables, grains such as rice, cracked wheat, couscous and pasta, and pulses like lentils, beans, chick peas, broad beans and split peas. All these ingredients fit well with today's ideas of healthy eating. You also find pine nuts, walnuts, almonds and pistachios in many dishes and dried fruit including raisins and sultanas, prunes and apricots. You find them even in meat, chicken and fish dishes.

"The cooking can be very simple and rustic because it is mostly a poor agricultural world. But it can also be very rich, elaborate and sophisticated because the area was the scene of very ancient and grand civilizations with powerful empires and glittering courts. Some of the dishes were developed in the courts of the caliphs of Baghdad and Damascus and of the sultans of the Ottoman Empire.

"One of the most appealing features of Middle Eastern cooking is the use of flavourings. The region was on the spice route since very early times. It was the transit area and the camel and caravan route for spices which were transported from the Far East and Central Africa to Europe. The middle-men who transported and dealt in the spices got to like their highly prized merchandise. Each country adopted special favourites and you can tell what country the dish is from by the flavourings. If you ever visit a spice street or a spice shop in a Middle Eastern bazaar, you will see bags of different coloured powders and collections of roots, bits of bark and wood, shrivelled pods, berries, translucent resins, bulbs, buds, petals, pistils, seeds, bottles of flower essences and great bunches of herbs. Almost everything that can give flavour or aroma is used for cooking.

"So go into a Middle Eastern store and explore. Ask what they are and you may be inspired to go home and cook something new. Just adding a tiny bit of a spice or flavouring will make an exciting difference to your usual food."

CLAUDIA RODEN'S BEID BI TAMATEM

(EGGS WITH TOMATOES)

SERVES SIX

INGREDIENTS
1 large onion, finely chopped
2 tablespoons butter or oil
1-2 cloves garlic, peeled and crushed
5 tomatoes, skinned and sliced (see Salsa on page 133)
salt and black pepper
6 eggs

1. Soften the chopped onion in butter or oil in a large frying pan.
2. Add the crushed garlic. When it turns golden, add the tomato slices, season with salt and pepper, and continue to cook gently until they are soft, turning once with a spatula.
3. Break the eggs carefully into a bowl and slip them, unbeaten, into the frying pan. Cook until set, season if necessary, and serve immediately with pitta or other bread.

The eggs can also be stirred gently until creamy and thickened, but I prefer to leave them whole.

Claudia Roden's Megadarra

Claudia writes:
"Here is a modern version of a medieval dish known as the food of the poor. An aunt of mine used to present it regularly to guests with the comment: 'Excuse the food of the poor!' – to which the unanimous reply was always: Keep your food of kings and give us Megadarra every day!

"The proportions of lentils and rice vary with every family. The caramelised onions are the main feature. With the olive oil they are also the main flavouring. In Lebanon they call it *mudardara*."

CLAUDIA RODEN'S MEGADARRA

SERVES FOUR

250 g (8 oz) large brown lentils
2 onions, finely chopped
125 ml (4 fl oz) olive oil
salt and black pepper
250 g (8 oz) long grain rice, washed
2-3 onions, sliced into half-moon shapes

1. **Wash and drain the lentils.**
2. **Boil them in a fresh portion of water to cover for about 25 mins or until just tender.**
3. **Fry the chopped onions in 2-3 tablespoons of oil until they are brown. Add these to the lentils and season to taste with salt and pepper. Mix together well and add the rice, together with enough water to bring the liquid in the pan up to the volume of rice.**
4. **Season again and simmer gently, covered, for about 20 mins, until the rice is soft and well cooked, adding a little more water if it becomes absorbed too quickly.**
6. **Fry the sliced onions in the rest of the very hot oil until they are dark brown and sweet, almost caramelised.**

Serve the rice and lentils on a large shallow dish, garnished with fried onion slices and with the oil poured over.

This dish is delicious served either warm or cold and accompanied by yoghurt.

* A tip: you may find it easier to cook the rice and lentils separately and to mix them together when they are both done.

* For different flavours add 1 teaspoon of ground cumin and 1 teaspoon of ground coriander to the cooking water, or 2 teaspoons of dried mint.

* In another dish of rice and lentils called *masafi*, the lentils are mashed to a purée. Red lentils, which disintegrate easily, can be used for this.

Claudia Roden's Lahma Mashwi/Shish Kebab (Grilled Meat on Skewers)

Claudia writes:
"Also called *shashlik*, this is probably the most famous Turkish dish, and it undoubtedly lives up to its reputation. It is said by Turks to have been created during the great conquering era of the Ottoman Empire, when Turkish soldiers, forced to camp out in tents for months on end, discovered the pleasure of eating meat grilled out of doors on open fires of charcoal or dry wood.

"The meat grilled on its own is delicious with only salt and pepper. In Greece and Turkey, quartered raw tomatoes and pieces of onion and sweet pepper are threaded on to the skewers in between the cubes of meat.

"The kebabs may be served in a flat, hollow Arab bread or pitta, with a salad of finely chopped raw tomato and raw onion.

"Alternatively, serve the skewers on a bed of parsley or chervil accompanied by various salads or, as is traditional in some countries, on a bed of plain white rice."

An added refinement is to marinate the meat first.

Here are three popular marinades for seasoning this amount of meat.

1 kg (2 lb) leg of lamb or fillet of beef, cut into medium-sized cubes about 2 cm (3/4 in) square:

LAHMA MASHWI/ SHISH KEBAB

SERVES FOUR

MARINADE 1

This is a particular favourite in Greece, where the distinctive flavour of rigani is much appreciated.

RIGANI: this is the Greek variety of wild marjoram. It can be found in Greek and Cypriot stores. An alternative is to use dried oregano or thyme.

INGREDIENTS
150 ml (1/4 pt) olive oil
juice of 1 lemon
2 onions, chopped and crushed to extract juices (this can be done in a garlic press or blender)
2 bay leaves, cut into small pieces
2 teaspoons dried rigani or oregano
pulp of 2 tomatoes, sieved (optional)
salt and black pepper

1. Mix all the ingredients together in a large bowl. Marinate the cubed meat for at least 2-3 hrs, or longer if possible. Iranian cooks marinate it for at least 12 hrs, which makes it beautifully tender.

MARINADE 2

from Sidqi Effendi's Turkish cookery manual:

INGREDIENTS
150 ml (1/4 pint) olive oil
juice of 2 onions
1 teaspoon ground cinnamon
salt and black pepper

Marinate the cubed meat as in Marinade 1.

MARINADE 3

INGREDIENTS
300 ml (1/2 pt) yoghurt
juice of 1 onion
salt and black pepper

Marinate the meat cubes as in Marinade 1.
This style of kebab can be served sprinkled with a little ground cinnamon.

COOKING THE MEAT

The method of cooking the meat for shish kebab is much the same, whichever marinade is used.

1. **After the meat is marinated, drain the cubes and thread them on to skewers, preferably the four-sided type.**
2. **Grill the kebabs over charcoal or wood, or under a preheated gas or electric grill, turning and brushing them from time to time with the marinade.**
3. **Cook the meat until the cubes are a rich brown colour on the outside, but still pink and juicy within. This takes from 7-10 mins, depending on the type and degree of heat, how far the skewers are from the heat source, and the size of the cubes.**

If you make these outside on a barbecue make sure that the fire has stopped smoking before you begin grilling.

When Robert was visiting Egypt in the late seventies on a very low budget he used to eat in the working men's cafés. At these cafés he would feast on ful (beans) and falafel or megadarra and muhallabia. They were so good he never even wanted to eat at the more expensive tourist restaurants.

FUL MEDAMES

SERVES FOUR

450 g (1 lb) ful beans, soaked overnight
1 tablespoon ground cumin
freshly ground black pepper
6 cloves garlic, peeled and minced

6 hard-boiled eggs, finely chopped
fresh parsley, chopped
4 lemons, quartered
1 large onion, thinly sliced
olive oil
salt

Preheat oven to 150°C/300°F/gas mark 2.

1. Put the beans in an ovenproof dish with the cumin, some black pepper and the garlic. Add enough water to cover the beans by 5 cm (2 in), cover and put into the oven.
2. Cook for 3 hrs or until the beans are very soft but not mushy.
3. Remove from the oven and leave to cool.

Put the eggs, parsley, lemon and onion in separate dishes and place on a table, together with a bottle of olive oil; use these to garnish the beans. Add some salt to the ful, stir in lightly and serve with pitta bread. This stew is much better warm rather than hot, and is also delicious cold.

FELAFEL

SERVES FOUR

225 g (½ lb) chick peas, soaked overnight and cooked for 1½ hrs
2 cloves garlic, peeled and minced
1 onion, grated
30 g (1 oz) fresh coriander leaves
1 teaspoon ground cumin
1 teaspoon ground coriander
½ teaspoon cayenne
½ teaspoon turmeric
½ teaspoon baking powder
1 egg, beaten lightly
juice of ½ lemon
flour
8 tablespoons sunflower oil

1. Blend the beans in a blender or food processor until they form a smooth paste.
2. Add the garlic, onion, coriander leaves, ground cumin, ground coriander, cayenne, turmeric, baking powder, egg and lemon juice and blend again.
3. Leave to stand for 30 mins.
4. Shape the mixture into small, round cakes 5 cm (2 in) across and 2 cm (¾ in) deep, adding a little flour and water if they are not binding.
5. Heat the oil in a frying pan over a medium heat and fry the felafel until golden brown, turning them over after a few minutes.

Hummus

Hummus is now an immensely popular dip in this country too. Why not make your own for a change.

HUMMUS

225 g (½ lb) chick peas, soaked overnight
3 tablespoons of tahini (sesame seed paste)
juice of ½ lemon
2 cloves garlic, peeled and crushed
salt
olive oil

1. **Cover the chick peas with water and cook in a covered pot for 2 hrs or until tender.**
2. **Drain the chick peas and reserve the liquid.**
3. **Mash the chick peas in a bowl, add the tahini, lemon juice, garlic and some of the cooking water and mix together well.**

Adjust the taste to how you like it by adding more lemon and/or garlic, and depending on whether you want a thick or runny hummus, adjust the amount of cooking water that you use. If you like a thick mixture, when you serve the hummus add a little olive oil to moisten it.

This goes well with some spring onions and some warm pitta bread.

Muhallabia

One of the Middle East's most common sweet dishes.

MUHALLABIA

SERVES FOUR

55 g (2 oz) ground rice
600 ml (1 pt) milk
2 tablespoons orange blossom water or 1 teaspoon vanilla essence
55 g (2 oz) sugar
55 g (2 oz) ground almonds
1 tablespoon chopped almonds

1. **Put the ground rice into a bowl and gradually add 150 ml (¼ pt) milk, stirring continuously until you have a smooth paste.**
2. **Put the remaining 450 ml (¾ pt) milk in a saucepan and bring to the boil.**
3. **Gradually add the milk to the rice paste, stirring continuously until you have a smooth mixture.**
4. **Pour the mixture back into the saucepan and heat and stir until it thickens.**
5. **Add the ground almonds and orange blossom water or vanilla essence and heat for 1 min, then pour the mixture into separate serving bowls and refrigerate until required.**

Sprinkle with nuts just before serving.

30 SOUTH EAST ASIA

Many different countries, each with its own history, religion and food, make up the region of South East Asia. In Thailand, most people are Buddhists and many are vegetarian, but pork, chicken, fish and sea food are also widely eaten. Malaysia is a multi-cultural society: the Malays are Muslims, but there are also large Indian and Chinese communities and Malaysian food represents all of these cultures.

Most Indonesians are Muslims, and because of their religion they do not eat pork or drink alcohol. Indonesia is the fourth largest nation in the world and contains over thirteen thousand islands, among them the Spice Islands that Columbus was looking for when he found the Americas.

This whole region has always been a focus for trade, piracy and war, with merchants and seafarers growing rich from the wealth of natural resources. Fertile soil, high rainfall and a tropical climate produce abundant harvests of rice, vegetables and many kinds of fruit.

The food and cooking of South East Asia are truly delicious. In most cities in Britain you can now find Thai, Indonesian, Vietnamese, Malaysian and Singaporean restaurants. If you have the chance try some of their noodle dishes, hot and sour soups with lemon grass, satays and many more.

Sri Owen was born in West Sumatra, in Indonesia, and now lives in London. She has given us these delicious recipes from her classic book *Indonesian and Thai Cookery*. They make a mouthwatering introduction to the food of this region.

Sri Owen's Babi Asam Pedas (Hot and Sour Pork)

Sri writes:
"There are different versions of this dish all over South East Asia. Mine is one that I used during the three years when I had an oriental delicatessen in Wimbledon; I know it works well, and my customers liked it."

SRI OWEN'S BABI ASAM PEDAS

SERVES FOUR

FOR THE PORK

1 teaspoon salt
2 teaspoons white malt vinegar
450 g (1 lb) lean fillet of pork, cut into 2 cm (¾ in) cubes

FOR THE SAUCE

4 shallots or 1 onion
2 cloves garlic, peeled
2½ cm (1 in) root ginger
2 large red chillies, seeded and chopped, or 1½ teaspoons chilli powder
120 ml (4 fl oz) sunflower or olive oil
6 tablespoons water
3 tablespoons white malt vinegar
1 tablespoon sugar
175 g (6 oz) can bamboo shoots, drained and rinsed
salt to taste
3 tablespoons fresh mint or basil

1. Rub the salt and vinegar into the pork and leave for 30 mins.
2. Put the shallots, garlic, ginger and red chillies into a blender, add 2 tablespoons of the oil and 2 tablespoons of the water and blend to a smooth paste.
3. Heat the oil in a wok or frying pan and fry the pieces of pork in batches for 4-5 mins at a time. Remove with a slotted spoon to drain.
4. Discard the oil, except for about 2 tablespoons. Heat this and fry the paste from the blender, stirring continuously for 3 mins. Stir in the vinegar and sugar and add the remaining water, the bamboo shoots and the pork. Simmer for 2 mins then taste, adding salt if necessary. Stir again for another minute, add the chopped mint or basil, stir and serve immediately with rice or boiled new potatoes.

This dish can be frozen satisfactorily. Thaw completely before reheating in a saucepan, stirring occasionally until hot.

Sri Owen's Pergedel Jagung Dengan Terung (Sweetcorn Fritters with Aubergine)

"This is a delicious snack, very easy to make, and as good for picnics as it is for parties. Some people prefer them hot, others cold, but I have never met anyone who doesn`t want more."

SRI OWEN'S PERGEDEL JAGUNG DENGAN TERUNG

Makes 15-18 fritters

6 fresh corn cobs or 326 g (11½ oz) can sweetcorn
1 medium-sized aubergine
salt
vegetable oil
4 shallots, chopped
1 red chilli, seeded and chopped or ½ teaspoon chilli powder
2 cloves garlic, peeled and chopped
1 teaspoon ground coriander
3 tablespoons rice flour or plain flour
1 teaspoon baking powder
2 tablespoons chopped spring onions
1 large egg

1. If you are using fresh corn, grate the corn off the cobs. If canned sweetcorn is being used, drain and put into a bowl, then mash it a little with a wooden spoon just to break the kernels so they won't pop when fried.
2. Cut the aubergine into very small cubes, put them in a colander and sprinkle generously with salt. Leave for 30 mins-1 hr, then rinse off the salt and squeeze out the excess water. Heat 2 tablespoons of oil in a wok or frying pan, and fry the shallots, chilli and garlic, stirring them for a minute or so. Then add the aubergines, stir, and season with the ground coriander and salt. Simmer, stirring often, for 4 mins. Take off the heat and leave to cool.
3. When cool, add the aubergine mixture to the mashed sweetcorn together with the flour, baking powder and chopped spring onions. Mix thoroughly and add the egg. Mix well again, taste, and add more salt if necessary.
4. In a frying pan, heat 5 tablespoons of oil. Drop a heaped tablespoon of the mixture into the pan. Flatten it with a fork, and repeat this process until you have 5 or 6 fritters in the pan. Fry them for about 3 mins on each side, turning once.

Gado-Gado

An Indonesian mixed vegetable salad with a spicy peanut sauce.

GADO-GADO SAUCE

SERVES FOUR

8 small dried red chillies
1 onion, grated
2 cloves garlic, peeled and minced
2 tablespoons peanut oil
45 g (1½ oz) creamed coconut mixed with
375 ml (13 fl oz) boiling water
170 g (6 oz) crunchy peanut butter (without added sugar)
1 teaspoon brown sugar
2 teaspoons lemon juice

1. Cut the chillies in half with a sharp knife and remove the small seeds.
2. Soak them in a little hot water for 30 mins.
3. Chop the chillies finely, mix with the onion, garlic and 1 tablespoon of oil.
4. Heat 1 tablespoon of oil in a heavy frying pan over a medium heat and fry for 5 mins, stirring occasionally.
5. Add the coconut milk gradually, stirring constantly.
6. Add the remaining ingredients and mix until smooth.
7. Simmer for a few minutes until the sauce thickens.
8. Leave to cool.

Serve with the Gado-Gado salad in a separate bowl.

GADO-GADO SALAD

450 g (1 lb) small new potatoes, boiled and sliced
110 g (4 oz) French green beans, boiled and refreshed in cold water
225 g (8 oz) shredded white cabbage, blanched
110 g (4 oz) beansprouts, blanched
110 g (4 oz) spring onions, sliced longways, or 110 g (4 oz) onions, sliced
225 g (8 oz) tomatoes, quartered
½ cucumber, cut in 2.5 cm (1 in) slices and quartered
1 lettuce, leaves separated

To garnish: 2 sliced hard-boiled eggs, pineapple chunks

Mix all the ingredients in a large salad bowl.
Serve the sauce and garnishes separately.

LAKSA

SERVES FOUR

900 g (2 lb) mackerel, cleaned and gutted
15 small dried red chillies, de-seeded, soaked and chopped (see recipe above)
2 50 g (2 oz) tins anchovies, drained of oil
350 g (12 oz) onions
2.5 cm (1 in) root ginger, chopped
2 cloves garlic, peeled
bunch of basil leaves
bunch of mint leaves
3 stalks lemon grass, bruised
2 teaspoons treacle
2 teaspoons lemon juice
salt to taste

1. Put the mackerel in a pot, cover amply with water and simmer for 20 mins.
2. Separate the flesh from the bones, discard the skin and bones and blend the flesh.
3. Blend together the chillies, anchovies, onions, ginger and garlic, add the blended fish and then return to the fish stock, adding some more water.
4. Add the basil and mint leaves, lemon grass, treacle and lemon juice and simmer for an hour or so.

Serve with rice, noodles or spaghetti. Follow the instructions on the packet for cooking time.

31 SPAIN

Unlike in countries such as France which had one cuisine for the rich and one for the poor, in Spain the food has always been a food of the people. Delicious onions and tomatoes, plentiful olive oil, fish and seafood, meat hot-pots and rice dishes make Spanish food an underrated delight. So if you've only ever tried watery gazpacho or leathery Spanish omelettes, you are in for a treat. Elisabeth Luard, the cookery writer whose book *European Peasant Cooking* is one of our favourites, explains how she discovered Spanish food through her children when they first lived in Spain.

Elisabeth Luard's Family Lentils

Elisabeth writes:
"You could say it was my four children who taught me how to cook Spanish food, instead of the other way round. This is because when my family was growing up, we lived deep in the countryside of Andalucia in southern Spain.

"My four children - the eldest was eight - went to the local school. They learned Spanish quickly (the littler you are, the easier it is), and asked questions about everything. Very soon they were coming home and telling me what their friends had for dinner, and could they please have the same? So, even though I was proud of being a good cook, I had to go and ask my neighbours how to make the dishes they described.

"At that time there were no supermarkets or ready-to-cook meals from the deep-freeze, and you could only buy what was sold in the local markets. Most of what was available was grown, cropped or caught locally, and all fresh food was seasonal. This was very exciting as you never knew what you would find in the market each week.

"There would be special cheeses which were only made in the spring. And the time when the new season's grapes arrived. The next week there might be big baskets of fresh olives, green and bitter and ready for pickling.

"There were wild crops as well - thistle rosettes which the country people like to stir into a stew, little tiny snails which you cooked in a broth flavoured with pennyroyal, mushrooms and wild asparagus which sprang up in the black patches where there had been a forest fire. We soon learned where to find our own.

"As we lived quite close to the sea, everything in the fish market seemed to be alive and wriggling: there were spiky-shelled sea-snails, slithery octopuses and long-legged crabs which looked like big scarlet spiders. The market people found it very funny that I had to ask how to cook everything before I took it home.

"Everyday meals usually had no meat. Most of our neighbours kept chickens for eggs and a few goats for milking. People grew Mediterranean vegetables - aubergines, peppers and tomatoes - as well as potatoes, carrots and onions. There were special paprika peppers which you hung up to dry, and fresh garlic (like fat white onions) which was plaited into strings and left to develop into juicy cloves. In the autumn there was the crop of chick peas and lentils to be hulled and stored for the winter.

"There were other things to learn, as well. I bought eggs and milk from the neighbours, but they gave me a little piglet to eat up all the household waste. He was called Greedy Piggy, and he lived in a sty at the end of the garden, where he got fatter and fatter.

"When the school holidays came round, we would take it in turns to make the evening meal. This meant that everyone had a chance to eat what they liked, and could show me what they had learned in their friends' houses.

"Everyone learned at least one dish - even Honey, the youngest, could make a mayonnaise. Her sister Poppy is now a chef in a smart restaurant, and this is what she makes when she's at home. It's a delicious lentil stew - still a family favourite. The everyday version I give here is vegetarian, but if you like a little meat, you can include chopped bacon or a bone from the joint (in my family this dish is called beans-and-bones).

"You can smarten it up for a party by serving little bowls of extras which people can stir into the basic stew. And there are lots of things you can do with the left-overs - even if there's no Greedy Piggy at the bottom of your garden!"

Poppy's Green Lentils with Herbs

"In Spanish this is called a *potaje*, and you eat it in a bowl with a spoon, and have big slabs of bread to mop up the juices. The bakery was next door to the school, and the bread was lovely - crusty and chewy and hot from the oven. The baker didn't use yeast - he kept a dollop of dough from the day before to make it rise. He started very early in the morning, and had a wood-fired oven which had to burn for an hour before it was ready to bake. He was so proud of his bread that he always pricked his initials on the end of each loaf. He had the happiest hens in the village - they were allowed to peck around the grain-sacks and under the table where the dough was kneaded."

POPPY'S GREEN LENTILS WITH HERBS

SERVES FOUR with left-overs

350 g (12 oz) greeny-brown lentils
3-4 tablespoons olive oil
1 carrot, scraped clean and chopped small
1 big tomato, chopped
2-3 cloves
1 tablespoon paprika
1 bay leaf
1 heaped teaspoon salt
3-4 cloves garlic
salt and pepper

TO FINISH:

1 large potato, peeled and cut into small chunks
250 g (8 oz) fresh greens (spinach, spring greens, peas)
a big handful of fresh herbs (parsley, chives, mint)
salt and pepper

1. Put the lentils and everything else except the garlic into a big pot with enough water to cover to a depth of two fingers.
2. Stick the garlic cloves on the end of a knife and turn them in a flame until the white covering blackens and burns and the garlic blisters a little. Drop the garlic (including the blackened skin) into the lentils - it smells lovely and sizzles as it goes into the water.
3. Put in the rest of the ingredients and a little salt.
4. Bring everything to the boil, turn down the heat, cover loosely with a lid and let it simmer for 45 mins, until the lentils are quite soft. Keep an eye on the mixture, stirring it every now and then, and add boiling water if it looks like sticking.
5. When the lentils are nearly soft, add the chunks of potato and more boiling water. Allow to continue simmering until the potato is nearly cooked.
6. Add the greens, washed and shredded. Bubble mixture up again and let it simmer for another 5 mins. Taste and season (you should always taste everything all the time).
7. Stir in the chopped herbs just before you are ready to serve.

Garnishes: For a party, accompany the stew with little bowls containing fried onions, fried strips of red pepper, chopped hard-boiled eggs, crisp cubes of fried bread, chopped raw onion, tomato, red peppers or grated cheese to be mixed into the stew. Some people like it with chilli sauce. And it's really good with a bowl of yoghurt mixed with grated cucumber - you drop a dollop into the hot stew and eat round it.

Left-overs: These are lovely fried gently in a big pan with a splash of oil until the juices are all dried out and it looks like a hash. Serve it with tomato sauce and a fried egg on top. Or you can dilute the left-overs with milk or water and liquidise to make a thick soup - delicious with fried bread rubbed with garlic. Or spice the left-overs with a little curry powder and use as a stuffing for pasties. Or mix with a beaten egg, cover with tomato sauce and cheese and bake in the oven.

NB Elisabeth Luard's new book is called *The Flavours of Andalucia* and is filled with her own beautiful illustrations.

Gazpacho

This popular recipe really needs good, ripe tomatoes. It involves no cooking just lots of chopping. It's perfect for hot, sunny afternoons when tomatoes are at their best.

GAZPACHO

SERVES FOUR

900 g (2 lb) tomatoes, peeled and chopped into tiny cubes
1 cucumber, chopped into tiny cubes
1 large green pepper, chopped into tiny cubes
2 cloves garlic, peeled and crushed
100 ml (4 fl oz) olive oil
50 ml (2 fl oz) wine vinegar
1 teaspoon salt
pepper to taste
450 ml (3/4 pt) water and ice cubes

1. Place all the chopped and crushed ingredients in a bowl together with the seasoning, oil and vinegar, and mix.
2. Add the water and ice-cube mix to taste, depending on how thick or thin you like it.

This gazpacho can be served straight away or left to rest in the fridge to allow the flavours to develop.

32 VEGETARIAN FOOD

This chapter is not last because it is least important. It just happens to begin with one of the last letters of the alphabet!

Although there are lots of vegetarian recipes throughout this book, we decided to include a few more here. They come from the ever-increasing number of our friends who prefer not to eat meat. With all the many vegetarian choices available, Robert and I could and often do exist happily without eating meat.

Vegetarianism has always been controversial and if you are vegetarian, you may find that some people, perhaps your parents, attack your choice not to eat meat. They may argue that you are putting principles above your health. To find out if there is any truth in this, we asked vegetarian cookery writer, Rose Elliot, author of the ever popular *Not Just a Load of Old Lentils*, to give us some tips:

Rose writes:
"Don't worry about balancing proteins: this is a modern food myth based on a misunderstanding of an idea put forward in a book called *Diet for a Small Planet*. When the author, Frances Moore Lappe, realised the confusion her book had created, she tried to correct it with the following statement in the tenth anniversary edition of her book:

> *In combating the myth that meat is the only way to get high-quality protein, I reinforced another myth. I gave the impression that in order to get enough protein without meat, considerable care was needed in choosing foods. Actually, it is much easier than I thought...[I] helped create a new myth that to get the proteins you need without meat you have to conscientiously combine non-meat sources... With a healthy, varied diet, concern about protein complementarity is not necessary for most of us.*

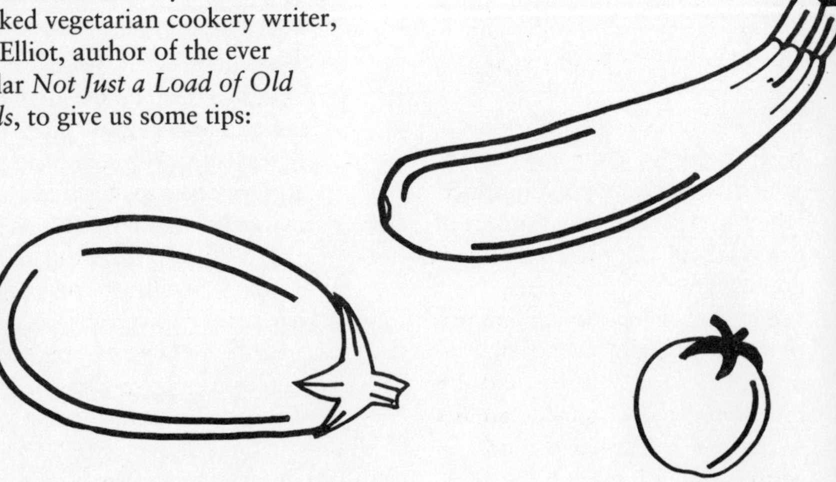

* If you (or your parents or doctor) are worried about your iron levels, make sure you're eating some of these iron-rich foods every day: rolled oats and other wholegrain breakfast cereals (some are fortified with extra iron)

- brown rice
  100% wholewheat bread,
- wholewheat pasta or wholewheat flour
- soya milk (use instead of cows' milk - unlike cows' milk, soya milk contains useful amounts or iron), soya yoghurt (buy at the health shop or make yourself with soya milk), tofu or bean curd
- all types of nuts – a wonderful natural convenience food
- sesame seeds and tahini (this is also in hummus)
- all the pulses, including chick peas and lentils
- eggs (the iron is in the yolk)
- dried fruits, especially dried apricots, but also raisins, prunes, figs and dates
- broccoli and other dark green leafy vegetables are also a good source of iron, and so, surprisingly, is the humble potato
- and the best news of all, plain chocolate even contains iron!

* If it is calcium you/they are worried about, it's interesting to note that, unlike animal products which are either a good source of calcium (milk and cheese) or a good source of iron (meat), vegetable products which are rich in one are usually rich in the other, too. So all of the foods I've mentioned above as being good sources of iron are also good sources of calcium with the exception of eggs. And, of course, dairy milk, cheese and yogurt are also rich in calcium (but do not contain iron).

* Getting enough vitamin B12 is the other thing people worry about, but it really isn't a problem. If you're eating some dairy produce, you'll be getting enough B12; if your protein is coming mainly from vegetable sources, just make sure you are including one or two products which contain added B12: breakfast cereals, margarine, yeast extract, textured vegetable proteins, fortified soya milk - read the labels!

Don't let anyone discourage you. There are millions of very fit, healthy, happy vegetarians in the world and vegetarian food can be absolutely delicious."

Here are Rose Elliot and her daughter Claire's recipes which they cooked for the *Eat Up* series:

Rose Elliot's Cheese Fritters

"One of Claire's favourite dishes and popular with all her friends (veggy and non-veggy). They like these served with home-made parsley sauce, chips for a treat, and a lightly cooked vegetable. Actually they're often not too enthusiastic about the vegetable, but broccoli, frozen peas or sweetcorn are usually acceptable, or slices of raw tomato, or matchsticks of raw carrot - for a special occasion these can be put together in a stir-fry (see below). The method may seem a bit fiddly, but you can do it in easy stages so you've only got to fry the fritters just before the meal. And they freeze very well after they've been coated with breadcrumbs: spread them out on a plate, freeze until solid, then put them into a polythene bag. Take them out as required and fry them slowly from frozen, making sure they get cooked right through to the centre."

ROSE ELLIOT'S CHEESE FRITTERS

SERVES FOUR

600 ml (1 pt) cows' milk or soya milk
1 small onion, peeled and with 3-4 cloves stuck into it
1 bay leaf
125 g (4 oz) semolina
1 tablespoon chopped fresh parsley
125 g (4 oz) grated cheese
½ teaspoon dry mustard
salt and freshly ground black pepper
grated fresh nutmeg
1 large free-range egg, beaten with 1 tablespoon of water
dried breadcrumbs
oil for shallow frying
slices of lemon
sprigs of parsley

1. **Put the milk, onion and bay leaf into a saucepan and bring the milk to the boil.**
2. **Remove from the heat, cover and leave for 10-15 mins, for the flavours to infuse.**
3. **Take out and discard the onion and bayleaf. Bring the milk back to the boil, then sprinkle the semolina over the top, stirring all the time.**
4. **Simmer for about 5 mins, to cook the semolina, then remove from the heat and beat in the cheese, chopped parsley, mustard and some seasoning — Claire recommends grated nutmeg.**
5. **Spread the mixture out to a depth of about 1 cm (½ in) on an oiled plate or baking tray. Smooth the top. Cool completely.**
6. **Cut into pieces, dipping each first in beaten egg and then in dried breadcrumbs. Shallow fry in hot oil until crisp on both sides, then drain well on kitchen towel.**
7. **Serve at once, garnished with lemon slices and parsley sprigs.**

Rose Elliot's Quick Parsley Sauce

"If you don't want to do too many things at once, you can make this in advance and cover the top of the sauce with a circle of clingfilm or wet greaseproof paper to prevent a skin forming. Then reheat it over a very gentle heat or stand the saucepan in a larger one with boiling water in it, over a moderate heat."

ROSE ELLIOT'S QUICK PARSLEY SAUCE

400 ml (3/4 pt) cows' milk or soya milk
40 g (1 1/2 oz) butter or pure vegetable margarine
25 g (1 oz) flour
3 tablespoons finely chopped parsley
salt and freshly ground black pepper

1. Put the milk, butter or margarine and flour into a medium-sized saucepan over a moderate heat, and whisk continuously until the mixture has thickened and become smooth - takes 1-2 mins.
2. Turn the heat right down and leave the sauce to simmer for about 5 mins, to cook the flour.
3. Whisk in the parsley and season to taste with the salt and pepper.

Rose Elliot's Favourite Vegetable Stir-fry

"You can put almost any vegetables into a stir-fry - choose your favourites! Cut hard vegetables, like carrots, which take a relatively long time to cook, into small, thin pieces, and softer vegetables, like broccoli, which cook more quickly, into larger pieces. Then you can throw them all into the pan together and they'll all be cooked at the same time. And it's fine if some of them end up quite crunchy.

It's fun to experiment with different colours, textures and flavours, and a stir-fry can easily be made into a complete vegetarian dish if you include one or more of the protein additions suggested below. You can also serve it with some rice, noodles or even mashed potatoes."

ROSE ELLIOT'S FAVOURITE VEGETABLE STIR-FRY

SERVES TWO as a main course or FOUR as a side-dish

175 g (6 oz) carrots
225 g (8 oz) broccoli
1 red pepper
175 g (6 oz) baby sweetcorn or frozen sweetcorn
2 tablespoons peanut oil
grated rind of 1/2 lemon
salt and freshly ground black pepper

1. Scrape the carrots and cut them into thin rounds or thin matchsticks.
2. Wash the broccoli, cut off the stems and slice them into thin rounds or matchsticks like the carrots, then cut the top part into

florets - not too small, as they'll cook quite quickly.

3. **Wash the red pepper, remove the seeds and stem, and chop the rest up into fairly small pieces.**
4. **Wash the baby sweetcorn.**
5. **A few minutes before you want to eat the stir-fry, heat the oil in a large saucepan or wok, if you have one, over a moderate heat, then put in the vegetables.**
6. **Stir the vegetables for 2-4 mins, or until they are just tender when pierced with the point of a knife.**
7. **Add the grated lemon rind, season with the salt and pepper and serve immediately.**

ADDITIONS FOR STIR-FRIES

FOR EXTRA FLAVOUR you can use sesame oil instead of peanut oil; you can also add a tablespoonful or two of soy sauce, a crushed clove of garlic or a teaspoonful of grated fresh ginger (add these with all the vegetables), or any chopped fresh herbs you fancy (add these at the end).

FOR EXTRA PROTEIN you can add drained, canned red kidney beans or chick peas (or any other types of beans you fancy); raw or roasted cashew nuts; blanched or flaked almonds, pine nuts or chopped brazil nuts; pumpkin, sunflower or sesame seeds; firm tofu, which is tasty if first sprinkled with soy sauce and some sesame oil, or fried separately before you add it to the stir-fry. (First stir-fry the tofu in your pan for a couple of minutes until brown, then remove from the pan while you cook the rest of the stir-fry. Put the tofu back in the pan when the cooking is almost complete.)

Chris and Ella's Marrow Goulash

This is a toothsome medley of vegetables cooked in baked marrow. Paprika and sour cream are traditionally used in the cooking of Hungary. Chris cooked this dish on our *Eat Up* programme for his daughter Ella and her Hungarian grandmother.

CHRIS AND ELLA'S MARROW GOULASH

SERVES FOUR

1 large marrow
170 g (6 oz) carrots, sliced
170 g (6 oz) parsnips, chopped
300 ml (½ pt) vegetable stock, made with a stock cube
25 g (1 oz) butter
1 large onion, finely chopped
1 red pepper, diced
110 g (4 oz) mushroms, quartered
400 g (14 oz) can tomatoes
110 g (4 oz) tinned sweetcorn
300 ml (½ pt) sour cream
4 tablespoons paprika, a mixture of hot and sweet
kitchen foil

PREPARE THE VEGETABLES AND MAKE THE STOCK

1. Peel the marrow, cut it in half lengthways and scoop out the seeds and pith from the centre. Leave at least 2-3 cm (*¾-1 in*) of marrow flesh.
2. Parboil the marrow by boiling it in water for 5-10 mins, depending on the size and age of the marrow – the greener the marrow the younger it is. The marrow should be slightly softer but still firm. Remove the marrow from the water.
3. Parboil the sliced carrots in the marrow water for about 8 mins, drain the carrots and reserve the water.
4. Boil the parsnips in the vegetable water until soft and ready for mashing. Reserve the vegetable water.
5. Use the reserved vegetable water and some stock cubes to make up 300 ml (½ pt) of vegetable stock. Follow the instructions given on the packet.

MAKE THE SAUCE

1. Heat the butter in a frying pan over a medium heat until the foam subsides.
2. Add the onion and sauté until transparent.
3. Add the chopped red pepper and parboiled carrots and sauté over a low heat for 10 mins, until the carrots are nearly soft.
4. Add the quartered mushrooms and mashed parsnips and cook for 2 mins.
5. Add the chopped tomatoes and sweetcorn, stir and leave to simmer for 25 mins.
6. Mix the sour cream with the paprika mix in a bowl and add this to the sauce. Stir until just heated through and remove from heat. Don't let the cream boil.

STUFFING AND COOKING THE MARROW

Preheat oven to 180°C/350°F/ gas mark 4.

1. Lay out a large square of kitchen foil and place on it side by side the two marrow pieces, middle side up.
2. Fill the centres of each marrow with the sauce.
3. Carefully bring the two pieces of marrow together to reform the original marrow shape, and wrap in the tin foil to seal it.
4. Place the wrapped marrow in the preheated oven and bake for 30-45 mins, until the marrow is tender.
5. Remove the marrow from the oven, open the foil wrapping and place the cooked marrow on to a preheated serving dish.
6. Sprinkle a little more paprika over the top, season with salt and pepper and serve.

Serve with rice and a green salad with pumpkin seeds.

The Old Moat Centre's Wholemeal Oat Biscuits

These tasty cookies are perfect to cook with young children and offer a healthy alternative to sweets. We filmed a group of four-year-olds making them for *Eat Up*. They loved every messy minute.

THE OLD MOAT CENTRE'S WHOLEMEAL OAT BISCUITS

110 g (4 oz) wholemeal flour
110 g (4 oz) rolled oats
110 g (4 oz) margarine
4 tablespoons apple and pear fruit spread (sugar free)
1 egg

1. Preheat oven to 190°C / 375°F / gas mark 5 and grease a baking tray.
2. Mix together all the dry ingredients, then rub in the margarine.
3. Beat the egg and then add this to the mixture to bind it together. Put the dry dough on to a lightly floured surface and roll out to 0.5 cm (¼ in) thick.
4. Cut out biscuit shapes and bake fo 10-15 mins on a high shelf. Put on a wire rack and leave to cool – if you can wait that long.

Paul Levy's Latkes

Originally from Kentucky, Paul Levy is one of Britain's foremost food writers. He recently presented the Channel 4 series *The Feast of Christmas* and has kindly given us this recipe from the accompanying book.
Since this is the last recipe in the book, we haven't adaptged it to our usual recipe format. It is just as Paul wrote it and presents a good challenge for your COOK IT skills!

Paul writes:
"I am very reluctant to give quantities for potato pancakes. Everything depends on the potatoes, and it is quite impossible to say what quantity of liquid any potato will give off when it is grated – even if you know the variety. None of the dozen or so recipes I've consulted even says whether a waxy or a floury potato is preferable. At least in America the all-purpose Idaho potato relieves the cook from having to make that decision. I have used both sorts of potato, and come to no conclusion about their merits. The cleverest recipes for latkes are those that try to give a potato/onion/egg ratio; but even those have to guess at the amount of starch – flour or matzo meal – needed to bind the mixture.

"So. Peel and grate coarsely (the food processor is a boon to latke-making) four large potatoes, weighing, say, 250 g (1/2 lb) each and one large onion. Put them in a mixing bowl and drain off most of the liquid. Add a generous amount of salt and freshly ground black pepper, and one large, lightly beaten egg if the mixture gave off a lot of liquid, two if it seems relatively dry. Bind with 1-4 tablespoons of medium matzo meal or plain flour. Some cooks add a big pinch of baking powder at this stage, some don't. Stir just enough to amalgamate everything. More liquid will begin to appear in the mixing bowl. Don't worry. The liquid will result in lacy, delicate pancakes.

"Heat a neutral-tasting vegetable oil in a frying pan until a haze appears. The quantity of oil is up to you. I use only a thin film of oil; others deep-fry their latkes. You can make small pancakes by stirring the batter and dropping it in the pan from a tablespoon; I use a larger spoon and make only three pancakes in a 22 cm (9 in) diameter frying pan.

"Like any pancake, it is ready to be turned when bubbles start appearing in the uncooked bater. Slide the spatula under and turn them, cooking for a few minutes – lift to see if the second side is getting crisp. Drain on kitchen paper. It is a counsel of perfection to say that the latkes should be eaten as they come out of the pan. Normally you will have to stack them up and keep them warm till the batter is finished up. They only get a little soggy.

"Some families eat these with apple sauce, some with soured cream. Traditionally, latkes are cooked in rendered chicken or goose fat, and they are, it almost goes without saying, divine with braised and boiled meat of every sort."

Further Reading

Here is a list of books which you should find interesting and informative. If you cannot afford to buy your own, then try your local library. The library will order books for you if they do not already have them in stock.

Second-hand and "charity" shops are also a great source of cheap cookbooks. Some are good and some of curiosity value only, but it's well worth looking around.

Apart from your local book shops, there are also specialist cookbook shops. We go to the excellent Books for Cooks, in London, run by Clarissa Dixon Wright, who is extremely knowledgeable and helpful and can recommend books on your chosen subject.

Darina Allen, *Food for Family and Friends*. Gill and Macmillan.
Sonia Allison, *Cooking Cajun-Creole*. Absolute.
James Beard, *American Cookery*. Hart Davis-McGibbon.
Simone Beck and Julia Child, *Mastering the Art of French Cooking*. Penguin.
Lizzie Boyd, *British Cookery*. Helm.
Jennifer Brennan, *The Cuisines of Asia*. Macdonald.
Catherine Brown, *Scottish Cookery*. Richard Drew.
Lesley Chamberlain, *The Food and Cooking of Eastern Europe*. Penguin.
Rose Elliot, *Rose Elliot's Vegetarian Cookery*. Harper Collins.
Rose Elliot, *The Supreme Vegetarian Cookbook*. Fontana.
Jane Grigson, *English Food*. Penguin.
Marcella Hazan, *Essentials of Classic Italian Cooking*. Macmillan.
Meg Jump, *Cooking with Chillies*. Bodley Head.
Mollie Katzen, *The Enchanted Broccoli Forest*. Tenspeed Press.
Irene Kuo, *The Key to Chinese Cooking*. Elm Tree Books.
Elisabeth Lambert Ortiz, *The Book of Latin American Cooking*. Penguin.
Elisabeth Lambert Ortiz, *Caribbean Cooking*. Penguin.
Sue Lawrence, *Entertaining at Home in Scotland*. Mainstream.
Paul Levy, *The Feast of Christmas*. Kyle Cathie.
Elisabeth Luard, *European Peasant Cookery*. Corgi.
Elisabeth Luard, *The Flavours of Andalucia*. Collins and Brown.
Sri Owen, *Indonesian and Thai Cookery*. Piatkus.
Claudia Roden, *The Food of Italy*. Arrow.
Claudia Roden, *The New Book of Middle Eastern Food*. Penguin.
Cora Rose and Bob Brown, *The South American Cookbook*. Penguin.
Evelyn Rose, *The New Complete International Jewish Cookbook*. Robson.
Evelyn Rose, *The New Jewish Cuisine*. Papermac.
Yan-Kit So, *Classic Chinese Cookbook*. Dorling Kindersley.
Yan-Kit So, *Classic Food of China*. Macmillan.
Colin Spencer, *The New Vegetarian*. Gaia.
Reay Tannahill, *Food in History*. Penguin.
Clare Walker and Keryn Christiansen, *A Taste of American Cooking*. Penguin.
Troth Wells, *The New Internationalist Food Book*. New Internationalist.
Hannah Wright, *Soups*. Hale.
The Cookery Year. Reader's Digest.
Larousse Gastronomique. Paul Hamlyn.
Mexican Cooking Class Cookbook. Windward.